BUENAS NOCHES BUENOS AIRES

Buenas Noches
Buenos Aires

GILBERT ADAIR

ff

faber and faber

First published in 2004
by Faber and Faber Limited
3 Queen Square London WC1N 3AU
This paperback edition first published in 2005

Typeset by Faber and Faber Limited
Printed in England by Mackays of Chatham plc,
Chatham, Kent

A CIP record for this book
is available from the British Library

ISBN 0–571–20611–5

2 4 6 8 10 9 7 5 3 1

for Bernardo and Clare

En Espagne, on orne la rue
Avec des loges d'opéra.
Quelle est cette belle inconnue?
C'est la mort. Don Juan l'aura.

*(In Spain, they deck the streets
With opera seats.
Who is this beautiful senorita?
It's death. Don Juan will meet her.)*

Jean Cocteau

The account which I'm about to write and you're about to read, an account, half calendar, half collage, of certain events in my past, which I'm typing out on a small olive-green Olivetti typewriter, is likely to be the last opportunity I'm ever going to have, before the brackets of my life are closed, to ask myself who I am, who I've been these past twenty-four years. Except for Dennis, I've never told anybody what happened to me and it will be his decision and his alone whether and when to publish – to try to publish, I should say – this text. If you, whoever you are, are now reading what I'm now writing, then it must mean that it has been published. So be it. I want you to understand, however, that whatever it may say on the cover this is not a novel, not even one of the so-called playfully postmodern type. Everything you read in the next hundred and fifty pages is true. Absolutely everything and absolutely true. This is a true story.

It was on the second of January, in 1980, that I settled in Paris. At the end of the previous year I had already made a four-day trip to the city to attend an interview for a teaching post at the Berlitz School on the boulevard des Italiens and, if the interview prove successful, which it was, to pre-book for myself accommodation on the Left Bank. I chose a top-floor attic room in the Hôtel Voltaire, overlooking the

1

Seine. Baudelaire had not only once lived in it – above the hotel's entrance there's an impressive brass plaque to that effect – but had written some of the poems of *Les Fleurs du mal* there. I was, as you can imagine, over the moon with Paris, with my new job, my attic. I purchased a copy of *Les Fleurs du mal* to read on the ferry taking me back to England and, when the boat-train steamed into Victoria, I used as a bookmark the embossed business card given me by Madame Müller, the hotel's owner, inserting it between its seventeenth and eighteenth pages. And there, so far as I know, for I must still possess the book even if I haven't set eyes on it for years, that bookmark is to this day.

My parents, who live in a pleasant two-storey house in Oxford – the Siamese twin, joined at the spine, of that to which it's semi-detached – neither approved nor disapproved of my leaving England. Frankly, they seemed little to care. The only thing we had in common was our blood kinship.

Did we even have that? I wondered. From my early adolescence on, I'd catch them peering at me as though they literally didn't know where I could have sprung from. (And, yes, I'm using the word 'literally' figuratively.) For them, as for their set of acquaintances, I was a real maverick, not bad-looking, it's true, and never downright unpopular, but a bit too ungiving and old beyond my years. Even my teachers, desperate as they all claimed to be for a spark of life from their lethargically sprawling pupils, probably felt I erred in the opposite direction. They found me too opinionated, aloof and judgmental for their own peace of mind, and I'm pretty sure they were secretly more comfortable with the loutish elements in the school who disturbed only the peace of their classrooms. (The fortnightly essays I would hand in to my English master, eccentrically punctuated and footnoted in Latin, Greek and Sanskrit, *à la The Waste Land*, never got the high marks I felt their originality deserved.) I was a throwback, said my father – but to what? A loner, said my mother – yet I did have a fair number of friends, though I was conscious I sometimes alienated even them. A timid soul, was my report card's conclusion, an appraisal that had me spluttering with rage. Something of a poseur, was the overall view. Which I suppose I was, except that, if you imitate something for long enough, you eventually turn into it.

In fact, that smart-alecky standoffishness of mine, the irreconcilability in my public persona of a brittle carapace with the runny soft centre only I seemed to know lurked within it – all I wanted was to like and be liked – was the source of most of my subsequent troubles. But I'm getting ahead of myself.

My father is a solicitor by profession; so I have to suppose he isn't a stupid man. Mark Twain wrote that, when he was sixteen, he was appalled by his father's ignorance and, when he was twenty, he couldn't help but marvel at how much knowledge that same father had succeeded in acquiring in just four years. When I reached twenty, I regarded my father as no less an ignoramus than ever, not to mention – it's a cliché, I know, for the younger generation to think so of its elders – a sexless, emotionless robot. An only child, I was amazed that this man who spoke so softly and so seldom I can now barely conjure up the sound of his voice, who read one book a year (which is, I liked to say to my pals, why he joined the Book-of-the-Month Club) yet spent whole Sundays poring over the *Sunday Express* from the first to the last page, news, sports, advertisements, *Gambols* and all, had even just the once aroused himself into the requisite state of physical excitation to produce me.

My mother I could still recall as youthful – relative, at least, to my own age – a living tree to whose warm tweedy bark I would cling like a koala bear while she chatted to some acquaintance of hers at a bus stop or else whisked me along the dazzling aisles of our local new mini-supermarket. (I had no matching memories of my father.) But the years had taken their toll, and she now appeared to me if anything the more melancholy of the two. It was almost as though she were relieved no longer to be young. (But she was only fifty-one or two at the time.) My callow conjecture was that, like most of her contemporaries, she had no sex life whatever, whereas, two decades before, they had had one – and she hadn't even then. Now that everything was levelling out, and would level out further as they all got older still, her jealousy of these contemporaries, of which as an adolescent I'd been aware, had started to subside. There are advantages to being old – and even dead.

I was to learn, in my late teens, from one of my two terrible twin cousins, Lex and Rex – obscene names I've ever after detested – who, eavesdropping on their own parents' conversations, would gleefully pass on any secrets which concerned me, that my father and mother had recently come close to divorcing but had decided to postpone the separation till my grandmother's death. (For some years now she's been what is called a 'vegetable', and I was once smacked at table for refusing to eat courgettes which, I protested, couldn't be good for you if vegetables were also wrinkly, smelly old people who wet their knickers.) It would be nice and novelettish to report that the marriage was to gain a new intensity from the enforced delay of an ancient parent's demise, for, as I write this, grandma continues to hang on in there; alas, it was not to be.

My father, I know, had no double life. But one day in the kitchen a tennis ball I was bouncing hit a join in the tiled floor and skittered off behind the refrigerator. Lying flat out on the linoleum, extending my arm as far as it would go between the fridge and the kitchen wall, I felt my groping fingertips graze some scrunched-up sheets of paper. I pulled them free, unfolded them (there were three of them) and found myself reading a misspelt photocopied text whose filthiness took my breath away. The author credited was one 'Onanymous', a joke I didn't get at the time, and the text itself was all 'big jugs' and 'throbbing cocks' and 'bouncy balls' and 'moist cunts' and 'yawning arseholes', an incredible verbal orgy that didn't shy from golden showers and outright scatology. I read the first page line after line, just glanced at the others, nearly fainted and hastily folded them up again (exactly as once, a dozy child, I had tiptoed downstairs for a glass of water in the middle of Christmas night, had caught sight of a pile of gift-wrapped packages beneath the tree and, well-brought-up middle-class little boy that I was – the presents were not to be unwrapped, not to be *seen*, until next morning – shut my eyes so quickly I lost my balance on the stairs).

I shoved the papers back behind the fridge, abandoned my tennis ball for good and, days later, would stammer whenever I had to make direct eye-contact with my mother.

There was one other factor, probably the most crucial, which prompted my decision to live in Paris. In my mid-teens I had a girlfriend, Carla, the youngest daughter of my English master, a prettier girl than everybody felt a weirdo like me deserved, of whom what I most vividly remember was her general *redness*. Her knuckles were red, her fingers were red, her hair was red, even her nose, which she would pick in public with the vigour of a chimney sweep endeavouring to dislodge an awkwardly located build-up of soot, had its reddish tip. I liked Carla, I enjoyed being seen with her, I thought her sexy, I thought her straggly sweater sleeves sexy – sleeves so long they obscured her hands right up to the knuckles – I even thought her redness sexy. (I never got used to the nosepicking, though.) I would take her to the Wimpy Bar on Friday nights, to the cinema on Saturdays and to an occasional school dance.

In the seventies, being a virgin at sixteen, which we both were – I mean that we were both sixteen and we were both virgins – was nothing special, nothing to be ashamed of. Nobody our age 'did it'. Or so I believed. Except that, in the light of what I now know about myself, I remember dates with Carla when she would look at me, after I'd kissed her goodnight, with an expression that seemed to say, 'You know, Gideon, you're a funny boy.' Oh, I didn't have to be told she expected more of me than that kiss, but I couldn't screw her on her own front doorstep, could I, so what was it she was waiting for?

The moment of truth came one evening when we were smooching on the sofa in her living-room. Her parents were out and I was allegedly helping her gen up for the following morning's French test. After little more than five minutes of lip-fumbling, she took my hand, insinuated it into the gap between two top blouse-buttons and left it clamped to her bra. Though I was shocked by her boldness, I dutifully poked about (her breasts felt both soft and hard, both cool and hot, to my touch); and when I realised I was actually toying with her naked nipples, I got as nearly erect as was possible in my tight underpants. But I realised something else as well. We had both fallen deathly quiet and what I realised, half-consciously, was that it wasn't just Carla's nipples that were exciting me but the lyrics of a number on a Chordettes' LP she had put on the record-player before we lay down on the sofa. *'Mr Sandman,'* it suddenly chimed in, *'bring me a dream,/ Make him the cutest that I've ever seen,/ Give him two lips like roses and clover/ Then tell him that his lonesome nights are over.'*

'Make him the cutest that I've ever seen . . .' I all at once knew, I *knew*, something about myself which I'd always known but had to be shown that I'd always known. I knew I couldn't conceal from myself any longer that I wasn't passing through the famous 'phase'. The phase was my life.

7

Like the Chordettes, I too wanted a boy with lips like roses and clover, a boy like blond, skinny, skinny-eyed, slightly dumb Gary, whom I'd seen one never-to-be-forgotten soccer practice day, wearing only white boxer shorts, hands cupped behind his head, stretched out the full length of a narrow wooden bench in the sports-ground changing room. I had been idly drying myself when another boy came marching up to him and, like a magician whipping a tablecloth off a dinner table without disturbing either crockery or cutlery, pulled Gary's shorts down about his ankles then yanked them off altogether. It all happened so swiftly I gasped. I couldn't believe my good fortune. Liberated like a genie from a bottle, his penis, which I had never seen before and which I observed was fat (far fatter than mine) and *café-au-lait* in colour, leapt up into the air and flopped back on to the delta of his abdomen like a trout slapped down on a fishmonger's chopping-board.

The moment it happened, Gary gawped at his exposed genitalia as though he were noticing them for the first time. He gawped, as well, at all of us boys gawping at him. Then he leapt to his feet, snatched a grubby towel from off the floor, wrapped it round his torso and only then – only when his big, fat, uncircumcised, adorably dopey cock, as thick as two planks, was no more than a shadowy protuberance on the towel's surface – was his lunkish confidence restored.

I had an erection then, too, I remember – it was a couple of weeks before my evening with Carla – but I told myself that, considering the fascination of nakedness, of anybody's nakedness, there wasn't a soul (or, rather, body) in

8

that changing room, whether straight or secretly gay, that hadn't. I told myself, just as the others had probably told themselves, that if I were a girl Gary was the kind of boy I'd fancy. Listening to 'Mr Sandman', though, I understood at long last that I truly did fancy him. There were no ifs about it.

I certainly wasn't about to assume there and then the implications of my new self-knowledge. I was confused, fearful of what it would all mean for me. I knew homosexuals existed. I was not so naive as to believe that nobody before me had ever lusted after somebody of his own sex. But the idea that I might one day exploit my desire, that I might actually *touch* what I'd seen (touching was as high as I dared to aspire), struck me as belonging almost to the domain of the miraculous.

Carla and I went on seeing one another, but a spell had been broken, a fact of which she seemed aware without, I hoped, tumbling to its source. There were to be, by mutual and tacit accord, no more smooching sessions on the sofa and fewer and fewer dates; until, just a month later, they petered out altogether without either of us openly confessing to being glad of it.

For the next few years I had three types of sex.

The first was masturbation. With the realisation of my true nature the floodgates were opened. I masturbated night and day until my penis's blood vessels felt tender and sore and ready to burst. Even if I did buy the odd magazine (always on a day-trip up to London, never at home, as though Oxford, with its God knows how many thousands of inhabitants, were a village so tiny that, no matter in which newsagent's I procured some sordid rag, news of my disgrace would fatally be relayed back to my mortified parents), the images that worked best for me were those culled from my own memory and imagination. The best of all, the image to which I would consistently return, was Gary stretched out on his narrow bench, his penis popping up into the air and, just as important for the satisfactory climax to my fantasy (why, though?), the look on his lovely face of disbelief that his sprouting animality had abruptly become public property. While feverishly tugging away at myself, I would revive that image of him as regularly as a theatre in need of a quick profit will revive some creaky but infallible old warhorse. It never let me down.

The second type was contemplation of Gary himself, on whom I had a crush for as long as we were at school together. Since, on his side, there was absolutely nothing, zero, zilch, nada, there was eventually, on mine, not much more than vulgar voyeurism. Though I had never been what anybody would call sporty, I suddenly took up – to the amazement, I must say, of my friends, all of them like me bookish sorts – soccer, rugby and swimming, not because I enjoyed them or was good at them (I didn't and I wasn't), but for the thrill of finding myself next to Gary in the changing room, since watching him put his clothes on aroused me now as much as having seen them being pulled off. It's strange – on the day I wrote about above, he dressed very guardedly after emerging from his shower, wearing a towel throughout his *toilette*, wriggling his underpants up under that towel and, like a bather on a public beach, removing it only when his trousers had already been drawn halfway up his thighs. Later, however, perhaps because he rather liked the idea that his body no longer held any secrets for us, he would become much more cavalier in the matter of dressing and undressing, cavalier to the point of exhibitionism. He would walk into the showers with a towel about his waist but unabashedly re-emerge with it slung over his shoulder. And there were times, ecstatic times for me, when, standing near me in his white undervest and nothing else, he would nonchalantly loosen up his genitalia with his right hand, jingling them like a pocketful of small change, before slipping into his soccer gear. In no more than a matter of weeks his privates had become his publics.

What most excited me about watching him dress was not just how he would put his clothes on – like everybody else, I realise – in uncannily the way you play a game of solitaire (blue shirt on white vest, brown leather boots on red socks) but also how the upper portion of those clothes (vest, shirt, school tie, braided school jacket) would be draped downward from the upper half of his body, over his shoulders, while the lower portion (pants, trousers, socks) would be tucked upward into all its snug clefts and crevices. When, in private, I reran the tape of this sequence in my mind, my masturbatory whimsies took a truly baroque turn. I would imagine myself playing neither his lover nor, as had sometimes been the case, his ravisher, but, and I blush to remember it, his anthropomorphised shirt (being his shirt, you see, would let me embrace, at one glorious go, his shoulders, shoulder-blades, back,

11

arms and slender, tender waist), his socks (being his socks would force me into mindblowing intimacy with what I suspected were his gamey feet) and, supremely, his underpants (the thought of being those heavenly white underpants of his, not just handling them, sniffing them, plunging my face into them, but actually *being* them, would cause me to ejaculate, in my fantasy, almost immediately on to his own astonished prick).

As I grew older, though, and turned nineteen, Gary and I parting for ever without either a word or gesture of farewell, voyeurism became as frustrating as it was ephemerally fulfilling and I determined to know at first hand what I had only ever dreamt about. That, at the start, meant getting up to London more often. Then, when I'd already decided I wouldn't go to university but, instead, find a job allowing me to live in Paris and, as I hoped and planned, become a writer, I was hired as an assistant in Foyle's bookshop.

In those dreary days London looked as though it ought to be sold off cheap at a jumble sale. It was tatty and unsexy. Piccadilly Circus, once the heart of the Empire, was now the backside – and it needed a wipe. But as I was to discover by surreptitiously riffling though a *Spartacus* guidebook in another department of Foyle's (I had been assigned to the performing arts), it did have a number of gay, or gayish, pubs – the Boltons, the Coleherne, the Salisbury – and a cluster of definitely gay discos, the most promising-sounding of which, off the King's Road in Chelsea, was *The Scarlet Pimp*. That was to be the site of my third type of sexual experience.

On my very first night there, it all seemed about to happen for me. The *Pimp*, as everybody referred to the place, had a minuscule box-office at street level, from which one walked down a sombre staircase to a dimly lit dance-floor and bar area. I had bought my ticket, had stuck it as requested on to my suit lapel (I was, it at once dawned on me, absurdly overdressed) and had begun to go downstairs, squeezing past a stream of mostly mustachioed young men, for it was the period of the clone look, coming upstairs, beefy and flushed, in teeshirts and jeans, with identically bulging crotches and identically shaped sweat-patches on their identical white vests, for a breather on the pavement – I had begun, I say, to go downstairs when I felt (I already felt!) the tap of a friendly hand on my shoulder. I immediately presumed a pass was being made at me. A pass, and I wasn't even inside the disco proper! But when I turned round, I was confronted by the fellow from the box-office. He was holding up a crumpled five-pound note – I'd given him a ten – and he did not display on his supercilious features, moustachioed naturally, the slightest interest in me either as a sexual object or simply as a human being.

'You forgot your change,' he said. So much for God's gift to gay manhood.

That night and those that followed I would disconsolately stand in the wings of the *Pimp's* dance-floor, rolling an ice-cold glass of Bacardi-and-Coke across my dripping brow, from left to right and back again, ignored by everybody, emitting the wrong signs, the wrong messages, the wrong vibrations, fanning myself with a cardboard bar coaster, feigning exhaustion from a surfeit of voguing, frugging or whatever was the disco craze of the moment, trying unconvincingly to convey the impression that it was out of choice rather than circumstance that I wasn't dancing. If I had to go to the club's lavatory (on whose sole unmirrored wall hung a huge framed image of a pallid St Sebastian, who looked barely more discomfited than if he were undergoing acupuncture), I'd behave just like the infant I'd been when catching illicit sight of the pile of embargoed Christmas presents. I'd strain to be casual but, glimpsing two clones noisily masturbating each other inside one of the cubicles whose door they hadn't even bothered to shut, or else, in another, also open, spotting a suede-jacketed youth on his knees servicing a man old enough to be his grandfather, I couldn't prevent myself from instantly closing my eyes as though I were guilty of an indiscretion, even if those open doors were sending out an unequivocal signal that the cubicles' lovers wanted to be watched.

I mustn't exaggerate, however. If through my timidity I missed a lot of the fun I saw being enjoyed around me, I gradually did start to be intrigued by these antics. What I took longest of all to get used to was the sight of two boys kissing. Just kissing. Fucking and rimming, fistfucking and cocksucking, all of them practices I thought of as hyper-masculine because doubly masculine, uncontaminated by what I already despised as feminine sappiness, I accepted as the potential norms (or abnorms) of my own burgeoning sexual orientation. Kissing, on the other hand, I regarded as the servile mimicry of a heterosexual cliché. I

14

thought it obscene (if you're a genuine vegetarian, you eat vegetables not nut cutlets) and the more affectionate the kisses the more obscene I thought them.

Nor, finally, do I wish to leave the impression that, when I departed for Paris seven months later (I worked at Foyle's till the following November), I had had no sex at all. Yes, despite an obstinately glum demeanour I could do nothing to eradicate – how many times in my life have I been told to 'Cheer up. It may never happen!' – boys would accost me, would chat me up, in *The Scarlet Pimp*. And as I had a room in a Bayswater flat which I shared with three other renters – a trio of straight, randily promiscuous students – and so couldn't take anybody back to 'my place', they would take me back to theirs, which were mostly bedsits, as I recall, bedsits or the next best thing. Without exception, though, these encounters were profoundly unsatisfying when not disastrous.

I wince at the recollection of two of them in particular.

The first involved a boy named Howard, twenty-two, a BBC trainee-editor with hippie-long hair, who invited me to his lower-ground-floor flat in Camden, where, no sooner was the front door closed, he peeled off completely, revealing on the dimpled dip of his abdomen the tattoo of a tiny tiger that appeared to stalk through the tangled grass of his pubic hair. Already stiff, he shoved his hand down the front of my new jeans and squeezed my cock sadistically hard. This sudden laying-on of icy fingers made me come at once, totally without warning, my penis erupting into the off-white cotton cup of my Y-fronts like an uncorked champagne bottle stanched by a waiter's

15

napkin. A scornful Howard withdrew his sticky-damp hand, muttering, 'Well, that seems to be fucking that.' Since all I could offer him was a strangulated apology that trailed off even before I'd finished it, he shrugged his beautiful naked shoulders. I hastily let myself out, aware that, as I slunk away along the harshly lamplit street past his pavement-level window, about the only part of me he would be able to see from inside his flat was the semen-stained crotch of my jeans.

The second encounter, with a Japanese boy, Yoshimoto, twenty years old and as lanky as a Harlem Globetrotter, occurred not at the *Pimp* but at Foyle's. A modern-languages student, Yoshi was trying to track down French translations of Tanizaki, Kawabata and Mishima, which he intended to read side by side with the original texts. I couldn't help him with that, but we got talking (in a sense – his English was almost unintelligible), had bacon and eggs in a fry-up café and took in a film that same evening. Yoshi was lonely in a city in which he had no acquaintances, either English or Japanese, and he clearly longed to be befriended. We saw quite a lot of each other in a harmless fashion, until late one evening, emboldened by more red wine than I was accustomed to, I suggested we go dancing. He seemed keen (I was the more nervous of the two), and he was also, to my relief, unfazed by the spectacle, on the *Pimp*'s dance-floor, of its all-male clientele.

For an hour or so we danced, though with not a *soupçon* of the violent crotch-groping which was going on all around us and of which, given how blatant it was, he couldn't have been unaware. It was, as it happened, a

Friday evening, one on which all three of my flat-sharers had taken themselves off to their families; and as Yoshi lived in Golders Green, in the far north of London, I ended by proposing untremblingly (the wine) that he spend the night in my room. Following some inscrutable ponderings, he agreed, we hailed a cab and were in Bayswater twenty minutes later. I had already decided that the time for the oblique approach was over; added to which, it was past midnight and the half-drunk Yoshi looked about to curl up and fall asleep on the floor. He collapsed on to the living-room divan, splaying his supernaturally long legs, a rungless stairway to paradise, over the carpet. I went into the bathroom and undressed. Then I took a deep intake of breath, walked back along the corridor and, now gratifyingly erect, stood in the doorway. Yoshi, who had been sleepily fiddling with the divan, trying, as I realised with a sinking heart, to figure out how it converted into a bed (it didn't), failed at first to look up. When he did at last, his eyes opened wider than I believed any Oriental's ever could. He opened his mouth wide too – to say only, 'Aw, *surplise!*' Then he gulped – I actually heard him gulp – and, crying, 'No, no, no, no, no, no, no, no! No unnerstand!', he gathered up his anorak, which he'd let indolently slide on to the floor, and exited both the room and the flat.

During the time I spent in London I had other experiences, most of them at least slightly less crushing than those I've described. All of which may strike the reader as pathetic, except that there are many more people in the world, whatever their sexual persuasion, who think of love without making it than there are people who make

love without thinking of it. In any event, after my preliminary trip to Paris, then my Christmas at home, when I
began packing for the definitive move immediately after
New Year's Day (and also, I might add, when I noted the
disappearance of a couple of gay magazines that I'd secret-
ed in one of the drawers of my bedroom chest-of-drawers
then forgotten about – so my mother and I were quits), I
could count on the fingers of one hand those very few sexual adventures of mine of which I had other than humiliating memories, the fingers of that same hand that had
laboured so much more effectively than any of my partners to arouse me. Feeling alone and unloved, possessing
neither roots nor branches, I couldn't wait to leave.

I arrived in Paris, as I said before interrupting myself, on
the second of January 1980 and moved straight away into
the Hôtel Voltaire. I'd given myself seven days' grace
before I was due to take up my post at the Berlitz, one day
of which was to be devoted to a probationary training
course (which went off without incident). The remaining
six I spent exploring the city that was to be my home for –
how long at that stage I couldn't have said, but I hoped for
ever.

It had been snowing before my arrival and there were
still cars parked in the streets sporting white crewcuts on
their bonnets, cut short-back-and-sides in the American
Marines style. It was cold and cheerless, yet it was also
Paris and even if in my first six days I spoke only to waiters and bank clerks and shop assistants in *boulangeries* –
why, I don't know, but I found myself ravenously gorging

on *pains aux raisins* and *croissants au chocolat* – I was delighted just to be there.

That first whirlwind week I visited the Louvre, Beaubourg and Sacré-Coeur. I opened a bank account at the Crédit Lyonnais. I bought a fake fur overcoat for myself at Kenzo's winter sales. I strolled up and down the Seine embankment as far in one direction as the Ile Saint-Louis and in the other as the Trocadéro esplanade. I went to the Cinémathèque Française to see René Clair's *Le Million* and the Comédie-Française to see Corneille's *Cinna ou la Clémence d'Auguste*, the most boring evening, bar none, I have ever spent in my life.

As a newcomer to 'abroad', I shamed myself three times.

In a brasserie on one of the *grands boulevards* I found myself on the receiving end of a waiter's sneer when I asked for the *steak tartare* I had ordered to be *bien cuit*. Later that same day, caught short in the rue de Rome, I sought relief in the Gare Saint-Lazare, in front of whose public toilets I queued up, fidgety as a schoolboy. When it came my turn, and I hurried into the cubicle, I discovered – nothing at all. Just a hole in the ground where the lavatory bowl ought to have been. Cursing my misfortune, I came back out again and, in my then hapless French, advised the next in line, a man I'd already noticed keeping an anxious eye on a car, his own, which was illegally parked on the station forecourt, that this particular cubicle was, as I phrased it, *complètement vide*. He stared at me as though I were mad, raced into the lavatory and locked its door. I waited smugly for him to re-emerge at once, unrelieved. Instead of which, my guffawing fellow-queuers and I were treated to an *1812 Overture* of intestinal explosions, shamelessly unmuffled, and I realised that if I were ever going to settle in France that hole in the ground was something I'd have to get used to. (I never have.) Finally, I had long been puzzled, during my ambulations, by loud appeals, nearly out of earshot, for somebody called François. 'François! François! François!' was what I kept hearing, and I would turn my head at crowded street corners, wondering who this elusive François was with whom so many people in so many different *quartiers* appeared to have urgent business. I registered at last who or, rather, what it was when I not only saw but heard a newspaper vendor on the Champs-Elysées. The newspaper he was selling was *France-Soir*.

By the week's end I could already feel myself going native. I had begun to buy *France-Soir* myself and was able, just about, to decipher it. Stubbing my toe, once, on the raised step of the doorway to the Voltaire bar, I yelped not 'Shit!' but 'Merde!', my first spontaneous 'Merde!' And when by Friday I'd received a cheque-book from the Crédit Lyonnais and written out my very first cheque, for a *pot au feu* at Lipp, I decided that, to celebrate the new, Parisian me, I would sign my surname's initial A, rearing up from my signature like a sudden leap on an anaesthetist's oscillograph, with a miniature Eiffel Tower. I still do.

The time has come for me to speak of the Berlitz and, specifically, of the peculiar atmosphere of its male common room: in the school's recreation quarters, I should say at once, the sexes were always segregated. In fact, during the four years I taught there, I was on more than mere nodding acquaintance with just one of the female teachers, a dark, spinsterish yet obscurely seductive Spanish woman, Consuelo – I never saw her complicated, hyphenated surname written down and never succeeded in getting my tongue round its pronunciation – and that was only because, having a coffee and cigarette one evening on the terrace of a café on the boulevard des Italiens which I used to frequent after classes (for a reason on which I'll elaborate later), I asked her for a light without realising that she was one of my colleagues.

So – the male common room. It contained all in all a long central table and eight chairs, a few other waiting-room chairs aligned along the walls and a cabinet of what we called our *casiers*, the locked metal safes in which each of us kept his 'things'. There were no pictures on the walls nor ornaments on the table, except for three chipped yellow Ricard ashtrays. Coffee, which was lousy, was obtainable from a distributor used by both the male and female staff and situated outside in the corridor that led to our classrooms. (The female common room, which wasn't officially off-limits to us males but which for some reason we treated as though it were, was directly opposite ours.)

Though there were teachers of every language, of every nationality, of every age, daily coming and going in the common room, most of them were no more than extras in my life. With the non-English-speaking faculty I remained on such superficial terms that I never advanced beyond the stage of reducing its members to a series of coarse and usually racist stereotypes. The Spaniards were the swarthy ones with Zapata moustaches, the Russians were the granite-jawed ones with garish string ties and cheap drip-dry shirts, the Chinese were the ones who looked Chinese. As for the French teachers (for there were some), none of them seemed to want to make close friends with expatriates who were unlikely to stay around too long, like those companies reluctant to hire overqualified candidates for a job they'll be bound to quit the instant something better comes along. It was only the English speakers whom I truly got to know; who became my first real friends in France; who, being in the great majority, had commandeered one entire half of the common-room table; and virtually all of whom, I was soon to discover, were gay. I discovered, too, that what had caused them all to fetch up in Paris, just as I myself had, was a not uncommon conflation, in those days, of two philias, franco and homo.

Among my compatriots and semi-compatriots (I mean Americans), four were to play an important role in the story I have to tell. There were others, sure, of lesser consequence to it. There was Chris Streeter, a Bristol-born boy with eyes as pink as a rabbit's and cheeks as rosy as a baby's buttocks, who'd already been nicknamed, long before my arrival, 'Christopher Street' after New York's envied hub of gay goings-on. There was Raoul de something, French-born but English-educated, broodily handsome, bilingual and bisexual. And there was Peter Hirschfeld, a young, shaven-headed American, homosexual but physically of no interest to me. (Also, he had one characteristic that drove me bananas. Wherever he might happen to live, it unfailingly turned out to be, by his own account, next door to the best butcher, the best *charcuterie*, the best *patisserie*, whatever, in Paris. This oneupmanship of his became such a tic that, whenever he moved, and he did a lot of flitting about, he would insist no less unfailingly that his *new* local butcher, *charcutier* or *patissier* was even better than the one he'd assured us had been the best before.)

But since, unlike the lives of those I'm about to introduce, theirs were never to be intimately interlinked with mine, I feel it would make better sense if I were ruthlessly to screen them out of my narrative and concentrate on the Big Four.

The doyen of the English staff, as he affected to refer to himself, always within quotation marks – 'Ahem, as the "doyen" . . . ' – was an American, George Schuyler. Schuyler (nobody ever called him George) was an individual of whom everybody in the school, myself included, grew fonder and fonder as we spent more and more time in his company but whom none of us ever really got to know. Even his age was a conundrum: it could have been anything between thirty-five and fifty. He was certainly gay – and was supposedly writing a novel when not teaching, a novel of which he would divulge only the catchy title, *The Quarterback of Notre-Dame* – but he never had the inclination either to confirm or deny the common-room rumour that he was the 'scion' of some colossally well-off Park Avenue dynasty (that surname) who had had to exile himself from the States in the wake of a hushed-up and most likely sexual scandal. He had, it's true, a patrician

23

veneer which sat incongruously with his also being an ill-paid Berlitz hack. That veneer, at least, we could see; as for what might be behind it, each of us had no more than his own personal hunch to go on.

Schuyler had been working at the Berlitz longer than anybody else; none of the older teachers could remember a time when he wasn't already the doyen. A half-empty paper coffee-cup and a copy of the *International Herald Tribune* in front of him, its crossword puzzle smudgelessly inked in, he was equally always there when you arrived, no matter how early the hour, like those people mysteriously installed when you enter a plane – their seat-belts fastened, their bags stowed away in the overhead lockers – even though you *know* you were among the first in the queue to board. His still boyish face was as endearingly crumpled as a seersucker suit on a muggy fourth of July. He invariably wore a smart, charcoal-grey blazer and a sometimes blue, sometimes pink shirt with a button-down collar and striped tie, the stripes diagonal. And he would say reparteeish things like 'Oh God, I've just split an infinitive!'; or, when you returned from a class after less than an hour, 'Short time no see'; or else, if you added 'No pun intended' to some remark that could have been misconstrued, 'And none taken, I'm sure.'

There was one thing which made him testy, and that was smoking. Since he chewed gum – or, rather, he moved his lips as though he were chewing gum, for I never once saw any evidence of the gum itself – he may well have been an ex-smoker. But several packets of cigarettes were consumed in the common room in a single day; the ashtrays, which regularly overflowed, were less regularly emptied; and as the day diminished, so did Schuyler's patience with the vile addiction. Considering his natural amiability, it couldn't have been easy for him to publicise his irritation. But by four o'clock or so, when even we smokers would start to find the fug sickening, you could see him peevishly waving a loose curl of smoke away with his hand; though, even then, he did it too late to have any real effect, like a back-kicking dog, unaware that its instincts have led it astray, trying to bury a turd under a cement pavement.

Schuyler was the least 'anecdotal' person I've ever met. Like everybody else – we would all talk about him a lot – I never ceased to wonder, given how well I knew him, at how very little I knew about him. Did he live alone or with a 'companion', a 'partner'? When he took (grudgingly, it always felt) a holiday, did he return to the land of his fathers, travel in Europe or venture farther afield? Did *The Quarterback of Notre-Dame* exist or was it meant to distract us all from what was really going on in his life? Did he even speak French? The unavoidable *casier* apart, I never heard him utter a word in the language, not even *merci* or *s'il vous plaît* or *ça va*, not even when it was called for (as when, addressing a teacher of another nationality, we'd naturally adopt the one language common to all of us); but it was impossible to believe that after living so many years in the country he didn't or couldn't or wouldn't.

The only story I heard Schuyler tell about his past was of his original arrival in Paris. It was in April 1968 and, just three weeks later, barricades had been raised, de Gaulle had disappeared and the country teetered on the brink of anarchy. And Schuyler? 'I was relaxed,' was all he would say, dry as ever. 'Sure, there were those barricades, but what do you expect of the French? I minded my own business.' What, though, we asked ourselves, was his business? *Mystère*.

A *mystère*, let me advise you, reader, that won't be resolved in these pages. There was to be no revelation, no second-act curtain line. George Schuyler was, perhaps, a Sphinx without a secret, and all the more enigmatic for that.

If Schuyler was, as I say, the colleague most present in my life, to the point where I cannot imagine my years at the Berlitz without him, I felt closer to another American, who, the son of an Iranian mother and a Canadian father, a diplomat at the United Nations, had the wonderful name of Fereydoun Fuller.

Fereydoun was short, dark, compact, soft-spoken and as mild-mannered as a superhero in mufti, one of those boys (actually in his early twenties) made sexier, more vulnerable, more rapeable, by having to wear glasses, itsy-bitsy granny ones in his case. His slimline ties were so long they plunged right inside his trousers (how far down did they go?) and his jet-black hair was always brilliantined. He was terribly polite. He would rush to hold a door open for you if you were carrying three coffee cups at once and apologise if ever you bumped into him. Schuyler put it well. 'Ferey,' he said, 'is the sort of guy who'd say "Bless you" if you farted.'

Unlike Schuyler, Ferey couldn't have been more openly homosexual and was my first real guide to the Paris scene. If we never became lovers, it was partly because of my own congenital shyness but mostly because I wasn't at all his type: as he once confessed to me, on that same café terrace where I made Consuelo's acquaintance, he had an incurable yen for men who were not only straight but actually homophobic, vicious gay baiters who would pulverise his pliant puniness under their boorish macho virility. The homosexual experience has ever been one of compromise but, poor Ferey, he was obliged more than most to settle for less than best, making do with married milquetoasts who fancied a walk on the shadier side of the street – of which, reader, I assure you that there are many, many more than you would believe.

Even so, what I found so singular about his sexual psychology was that for a masochist, which he literally was, for somebody who routinely fantasised about having his little bronzed body mangled by thuggish goons with necks as thick as thighs, he was also an incorrigible hypochondriac, one whose motto in life, inherited from his mother, was 'There's no such thing as a safe mole.'

You would forever find him fretting over which of his many pills to pop and when. My suspicion was that he was even – and this I'd never come across before nor ever have since – a *dental* hypochondriac. No matter when you spoke to him, he had either just had an appointment with his dentist or else another was looming. Since, in spite of the fact that his teeth looked fine to me, he went so often, I can't believe he didn't look forward to it. Yet, one evening, when I picked him up in his studio apartment in a side street not far from the place de la Bastille (we were off to the theatre together), and he asked me if I wanted to see an image of his ideal lover – of course I did – what he showed me was a snapshot clipped from an American wrestling magazine. This ideal lover, a bald, black-masked, grotesquely obese bruiser, stage name 'Attila the Hunk', bulged every which way out of his torso-hugging costume, but what caught my eye was the ugly crossword-puzzle grin visible through his mask's scary mouth-slit.

Ferey also had, hanging up in his apartment, and directly facing its front door, so that it was what you encountered the instant you stepped inside, a large print of Robert Mapplethorpe's 'The Man in the Polyester Suit', the photograph of a black man wearing the titular three-piece suit out of whose open flies protruded a penis of Zeppelin-like proportions. 'Zeppelin', certainly, was the word which crossed my mind when I took a quiet moment to study it. I thought of the newsreel footage of the Hindenburg airship crash over New York in 1937 and the newsreel commentator's famous 'Oh! the humanity!' That's what I said to myself too – Oh! the humanity! – as I gawked at the size of the black man's prick. (When, this first time I entered his apartment, thinking to be clever, I remarked, 'That photograph's well-hung', Ferey gave me the sort of look that suggested I was about the sixty-third visitor to have made the same joke.)

He was, finally, exasperatingly faddy about food. He wasn't quite a vegetarian – that would have been too cut-and-dried – but he would fuss over the precise composition of a dish, even in the kind of inexpensive restaurants we all ate in, restaurants whose waiters and waitresses had never in their lives been asked whether there were almonds in the curry or whether the skin could be removed in advance from the roast chicken. He – Schuyler, rather – once made the common room roar. We were talking about sex, as per usual, and Ferey piped up (and, as I now recall his voice, 'pipe' is what it did) that he would try anything once except eat human excrement. 'Eat human excrement?' Schuyler exclaimed in mock-shock. 'You won't eat raisins!'

The third of my Musketeers was an Englishman calling himself Mick Morrison. Mick, however, I took a long time to warm to despite his many kindnesses to me. For a while I thought him fundamentally bogus, the sort of bullshitter who, at twenty-five, claims he won't survive thirty, at thirty-five that he won't survive forty, etc., etc., decade after decade, until he dies in his bed an octogenarian. (Perhaps, too, I always knew he'd be the first, as he was, to see through my own phoney façade.) His name, I discovered, peeking at his passport one day when it itself was peeking out of the decrepit overnight bag he carried over his shoulder at all times, wasn't Morrison at all but Hurdle, Michael Hurdle, born, improbably, in High Wycombe. Since rock was one of his passions – his feet propped up on the common-room table, he would never not be swaying, gyrating, snapping his nasty nicotiny fingertips, the filter tips of his long, bony, cigarette-slim fingers, to unheard melodies – I assumed he'd chosen the name of 'Morrison', intrinsically less memorable as it surely is than 'Hurdle', as a tribute to either Jim or Van, just as 'Mick', instead of 'Michael' or 'Mike', was likely intended as a homage to Jagger.

In his mid-thirties, he had the precociously stooped and streaky appearance of somebody who has spent too much of his life in a pop-music milieu. His thinning hair was worn shoulder-length, his chin was permanently stubbly and, except during a freakish heatwave one July, when the common room windows were left open all day for the first time in living memory, he would always turn up sporting a long black cloak lined with scarlet satin, one which lent him, as it was meant to, a cod-Draculaesque air. Altogether, Mick toiled industriously at being thought of by those around him as a demonic individual, snapping shut, for example, if ever you chanced to walk past him, a dog-eared diary he'd been writing in, even though you hadn't the least interest in learning what it might contain.

To be fair to him, I must admit that – while it was with Ferey I explored the city's respectable homosexual clubs (the *Fiacre* on the rue du Cherche-Midi, the oldest-established of all and by my time deadly square; the *Nuage*, off the place Saint-Germain; the *Bronx*, rue Sainte-Anne; the *Soledad*, rue du Dragon; and the trendiest, so trendy we were turned away more often than we ever squeaked in, the *Palace*, faubourg Montmartre), with him, too, I spent a package-deal weekend in London where we shared a chaste king-sized bed in a lugubrious Paddington B-&-B and where he, a foreigner, introduced me to the most congenial of the local dives (the pis-elegant *Rockingham* in Soho, with its snooty Cardin-suited gigolos, smooth rather than rough trade; a raunchy club called *Heaven* in the Charing Cross Road; the King William IV pub in Hampstead, none of which I'd ever been to when I was briefly London-based) – it was Mick, generously, I can see now, for I held no interest for him as a prospective sexual partner, who let me hang out with him on some of his regular 'descents' (his word) into what he was also pleased to define as the 'underbelly' of the Parisian gay scene.

He was an indefatigable cottager. He knew all the best and busiest of Paris's *pissotières*, even the very one, still reekingly extant, which, a century before, the composer Saint-Saëns would visit in the morning carrying a loaf of fresh bread – which he left hidden out of sight beneath one of the urinals – then revisit the same evening to retrieve the *baguette*, now porous with pee, with which, in the plush fastness of his *hôtel particulier*, he got up to who knows what deliriously disgusting pranks. Mick also took me to bathhouses and seedy saunas and seedier porn cinemas, where he would breezily pull out his cock, as plump, cylindrical and symmetrical as a pepper-pot in a pizzeria, and start to masturbate in front of me without so much as a by-your-leave. And he invited me once to accompany him on an excursion, one wintry Sunday afternoon, to that perennial cruising ground, the Jardin des Tuileries.

Was the excursion a success? I can't speak for Mick, though he vanished from my view in no time at all and, next morning at the Berlitz, treated me to a horrible sidelong leer. For me it might have been judged a half-success since, cruising for the first time in my life, I had an interesting afternoon but one which ended, as ever, by my going home alone.

As I experienced it, cruising was less a moveable feast than a moveable fast, an exchange of glances replacing instead of foretokening an exchange of caresses (or even phone numbers). Except that, when I write 'as I experienced it', I do myself an injustice. The fact is that, in those leafless, lifeless gardens which looked on to the place de la Concorde, lifeless, that is, except for two or three dozen cruising gay men, nobody, nobody at all, not just I, picked up anybody else. Or so it appeared to me. If they did (which I suppose they must have done, otherwise why would they bother going again and again?), when and how did it happen? It was as though immediately hitting the jackpot would have been to win the game too quickly, thereby negating the thrill, the very *raison d'être*, of the pursuit; as though, even if the hopes of each and every one of my fellow-cruisers were ultimately pinned on being paired off, none of them cared for it to happen *just yet*. That theory, certainly, would account for the distance they all took care to maintain from one another throughout the long afternoon. Watching them soundlessly dart from tree to tree, turn away from the world for a brief moment to light up a cigarette, disappear behind – then suddenly reappear from behind – the museum of the Orangerie, was like watching the courtship of statues.

Yet somehow, somewhere, at some time, unobserved by me, these statues did make contact and did go off together two by two, while I went home alone to my room in the Voltaire. Again, *mystère*.

And so we come to Ralph, Ralph Macavoy, so cute and baby-faced that fondling his privates – and my lecherous fingers instantly craved to get, so to speak, their hands on them – would have been like seducing Cupid himself. 'Mr Sandman, bring me a dream,/ Make him the cutest that I've ever seen . . .' Ralph, oh, Ralph *was* the cutest that I'd ever seen, my own ideal lover, without whose ravishing presence Paris for me would have seemed as perpetually deserted as Paris in August.

My eye was drawn to him on my very first day in the Berlitz common room. A Londoner, he was twenty-five but looked sixteen. He had thick black hair and a luscious lower lip which could have served as a model for a Dalinian sofa and on which I'd have loved to curl up and fall asleep. He was short, even stocky, yet he had the sort of soft, quasi-feminine features we associate with an androgynous torso and lean, long legs. By some that combination – stockiness and ethereality – would have been judged ungainly. To me it was, I repeat, perfection. For the first time I didn't just want to fuck somebody of my own sex but to *kiss* him, to drench him with kisses, suffocate him with kisses, kill him with kisses. I dreamt of kissing him on the palm of his hand, on his wrist, along his arm up to his elbow and beyond, I dreamt of kissing him the entire length of that arm with the same lip-smacking relish as I'd eat a corn-on-the-cob!

Calm down. Come back to earth. *Piano, piano.*

No, no, Ralph really was marvellously cute. He'd walk into a crowded gay bar, scan the room for somebody who caught his fancy, march right up to the chosen one and, dispensing with all the coded, time-honoured preliminaries, as though it never crossed his mind that he might be rejected, say, 'I want to be fucked by you.' And, inevitably, he would be.

For a time there, I was insanely jealous (ah, unrequited love – the root canal of the soul) of every man and boy Ralph slept with, of anybody at all in his good graces, of anybody with whom he exchanged a word. I was jealous of Pippa the long-haired dachshund who pined for him back in Chiswick, of the *dramatis personae* of his wet dreams, of the very noodles, especially those gossamer Chinese ones the French call *cheveux d'anges*, that his tongue, like an anteater's, would slurp up past his glossy teeth and deliver deep into his throat – a single deft whoosh! and they were gone. Of course I never did succeed in 'having' him. Not only was there, in the background, some sort of boyfriend – a wealthy, middle-aged protector was what we all imagined, for Ralph was the only one of us to possess a car of his own, even if it looked like a second-hand vacuum cleaner, and, in general, he had more money to throw around than might have been expected of an impecunious English-language teacher – but also, I insist, he was just such a dish he could have had anybody he wanted.

The closest I came to something resembling sexual contact with him was his letting me one evening, as I made a detour to the lavatory before quitting my classes for the day, burst in front of the mirror a pimple which had materialised on the fleshy little bridge between his nostrils and which he couldn't get a handle on unaided. (When I stepped into the lavatory, his eyes were already watery from a series of botched experiments.) But even I, candid as I have been, must draw the line at rhapsodising on the nerdish erotics of pimple-popping. All I'm willing to say is that, when Ralph's pimple burst – discharging on my thumbnail a tiny tubular pellet of toothpaste-white pus – so did I. Thank God I was on my way home.

Though there was, as you would expect, a high turnover in the Berlitz, sudden arrivals and sudden departures, teachers who didn't clock in one morning, or any other morning after, without having hinted in advance that they might have reached some kind of an interim climax in their careers, it was an environment in which I personally thrived. It's true that I'd complain of my lot just as much as any of the older hands – the dismal pay, the day-in day-out drudgery, the unattractiveness of too many of my students. Yet not since childhood had I felt so (there are no other words for it) *at home*. When I really had been at home, a teenager in Oxford, I'd felt, rather, as though I were adrift. I'd had nobody to speak to about my apprehension of my sexual nature and my incomprehension of what I would only later discover was its comparative normality. (I know now that homosexuality is the most normal – oh well, yes, the *second* most normal – thing in the world.) And at Foyle's, whose turnover was even more rapid than at the Berlitz, I was employed for so short a period I didn't give myself enough time to overcome my own innate timorousness. It may be hard to believe, for it was a dead-end job with unsociable hours, no future and next to no money, but the Berlitz gave my life a meaning. For once I had to be somewhere, I was expected, I would be missed if I weren't there.

It didn't happen at once. To start with, shy as I continued to be, convinced as I still was of my physical and social inadequacy, what my new life brought me was just my old loneliness in a new setting. In my first few weeks in Paris I had nowhere to go after my last class of the evening save, by my eternal self, following a solitary supper in the sort of anonymous (and onanymous) brasserie that was willing to humour loners and losers, to my room in the Voltaire, so woebegone I felt like hanging a cardboard sign, *Prière de Déranger* or *Do Disturb*, on my outside door handle.

Apropos of which there occurred a droll encounter at the hotel, no more than a couple of months after I'd moved in. The Voltaire had a night porter, a Tunisian of indeterminate age, whose features were obliterated by the blackest-rimmed pair of spectacles I have ever seen and who, behind the reception desk, was always nose-deep in a book. Though I was initially impressed by what I took to be his laudable ambition to better himself, I soon learned to my cost, for I once made the polite point of asking what he was reading, that he was a fanatical devotee of every bestselling conspiracy theory to have circulated the globe since the year dot. No matter how desirous I was for human company, I swiftly learned to steer clear of engaging with him, since, if ever I did, it would take me all of half-an-hour to get free of him and twice as long again to cleanse my brain, now nearly as addled as his, of UFOs, Pharaonic curses, the Cathar heresy, the secret treasure of the Templars and the Carolingian dynasty of Christ.

One evening, on my way out to the cinema, I stopped in the lobby to stroke Bobby, Madame Müller's aged, incontinent labrador, who would be parked there for the night out of too much harm's way and who would woozily peer up at me through the spiders' webs infesting his glaucoma-stricken eyes. Then I groped inside my overcoat pocket for my doorkey, which I had to surrender to the porter before leaving the hotel.

As I did, he glanced up at me from whatever mumbo-jumbo he was reading at the time and enquired what I was looking for.

'My key,' I replied, sticking my forefinger down through the pocket's holey lining.

For a second or two he remained silent. Then he said, 'Seriously, though, isn't it you yourself you're looking for?'

I stared at him, discombobulated by the question's fatuity, wondering if even in the weird, warped world he inhabited it really might be possible to find yourself in the lining of an overcoat. Then I felt my fingertip brush against the cold metal key-ring. I carefully drew it up to the surface through the largest and most easily manoeuvrable of the holes and, handing it over to him, said coolly, 'No, I wasn't looking for myself. I was looking for my key. And here it is.'

Yet, minutes later, strolling along the boulevard Saint-Germain, I realised the moron was right after all. I *was* looking for myself.

How at that instant I hated everybody whose path I crossed, how I hated all those people going places together, in the opposite direction, always in the opposite direction, all those couples staring at me out of their four cold little eyes, arms linked, destinies linked, talking, smiling, laughing, taking each other's presence for granted and rowdily elbowing me out of their joyous way, while I alone seemed to be living out of conformity, living because living is what you're expected to do if you're alive. (When in Rome . . .)

Those were bad days for me, days when I almost thought of packing it in and returning to England, days when I'd actually hover outside the Berlitz's personnel office, ready to resign on the spot. I persevered, though, I *had* to persevere; and little by little I discovered that for all the differences separating me from my fellow-teachers – differences of appearance, nationality, background, age and class – we had one thing in common. We were all expatriates, and expatriates are compatriots, possessed of their own customs, traditions, history and language. (English, fortunately for me, has always been the expatriate's native tongue.) I discovered, too, that what makes expatriates compatriots is precisely those differences, ones which in other circumstances would conspire to segregate us. We were singled out, wittingly or not, by our estrangement from the shared heritage of the country of which we were the guests, a heritage from which, no matter how much we kidded ourselves, we were also excluded.

I won't say that from that point on I wished to be at the Berlitz more than anywhere else in the world. It was a grim business rousing myself on a pitch-dark winter morning; grim, uncoiling my drowsy carcass from bed and dragging it to the Saint-Germain-des-Prés metro station; grim, the journey across town in a stuffy, steamed-up compartment dense with uncaptioned faces and, underneath their overcoats and windcheaters, unfathomable bodies; grimmest of all, the first class of the day. Yet, two hours later, Paris was alive and humming, and so was I. Whether gulping down a palate-scalding coffee, or simply walking to and from my classrooms, saluting colleagues as they went about their own daily rounds, I felt I belonged somewhere at last, belonged in as much a social as a professional sense.

Nothing could have been more reassuring to me than the sight of Schuyler, coffee cup and *Herald Tribune* in front of him, forever on duty before any of the rest of us, overseeing his brood with a benign and tranquil tyranny, like a vigilant lioness her cubs, inviting us to share his pleasure in a nifty crossword clue ('Scratch Pad' is one I remember, for which the four-letter answer was – think about it for a moment – 'Hell'). Reassuring, too, was the babel of the common room, a jangling pandemonium not of different languages but of different accents, a babel outroared in its turn by the clamour of the bells that would summon us, the whole day long, to our various classes.

Those classes now. The self-styled 'Berlitz Method' disallowed us, even with total beginners, from addressing our students in any language but the one we were teaching them. So inviolable was this injunction that the strictness of our adherence to it was monitored by a microphone in every classroom, and it resulted in our needing forever to drive home some elementary point when it would have taken so much less time to say 'Votre nom, s'il vous plaît?' or 'Ouvrez vos cahiers à la page vingt-huit' before immediately reverting to English. The students would have preferred it too. Many of them, too many of them for my taste, were middle-aged businessmen and women, avid to get on, to cram into an hour's session as much as could possibly serve them in their careers, impatient with anything as frivolous as adjectives or adverbs, and scandalised that in order to convey the meaning of the word 'sleep', say, I was forced – rather than merely scrawling 'sleep = sommeil' on the blackboard – to cup the palms of my hands under my chin and close my eyes and even, for the benefit of the real, unteachable dodos, pretend to snore.

There were compensations. Whenever I strode into any new class, the first thing I did – as, I learned, did most of my gay colleagues – was scrutinise the half-dozen faces nervously gazing up at me to discern whether at least one of them would make the coming lessons more than just bearable; whether, among my captive audience, there was one youthful set of features (I never dared to pray for more than one per class) I could guiltlessly contemplate, as also a youthful body I could attempt mentally to strip, while going through the mechanical motions required of me by my employers. It became standard with me, too, without fail, September after September – the start of our teaching year coincided with the *rentrée universitaire* – to come to the premature conclusion that, *oh God*, this year there's *nobody*. Premature, because, as the days and weeks ticked by, and each of the semicircle of faces was endowed with individual expression and personality, there was always, *always*, at least one of them I would surprise myself by finding sexy and beautiful, even if I wouldn't have looked twice, and hadn't looked twice, the first time around.

In the opening session I confined myself to 'drawing out' my students, inviting them to talk about their lives and backgrounds. All of which was in accordance with my training as a Berlitz teacher, except that I enjoyed privately thinking of it as a cunningly flirtatious gambit I myself had devised, like the central conceit of Agatha Christie's whodunnit *The ABC Murders*, whose villain, saddled with an all too deducible motive for doing away with somebody bearing the initials C.C., camouflages his homicidal intentions under the cloak of a serial killer's insanity by murdering an A.A., then a B.B., and then, and only then, the person he intended to murder in the first place. For me it became the means by which, under cover of the Berlitz Method, I could pump the one boy (it was always a boy) whose background genuinely interested me. That the petite, lavender-scented Monégasque girl had an elder sister who played the violin in an internationally famous string quartet, that the Belgian paediatrician had lived two of his teenage years just around the corner from Edinburgh Castle, were random scraps of information no sooner received than ignored, in one ear, out the other, significant only in that they enabled me finally to turn to the real object of my interrogation, as though he were haphazardly next in line, and invite him to tell us – tell me, rather – something about himself.

I would even experience a faint frisson whenever I set my class a written test, as we were all instructed to do once a month, and leaned suggestively over the hunched shoulders of some beetle-browed beauty, rubbing my wrist, accidentally on purpose, as we used to say at school, against his naked knuckles, while pointing out one of his poignant misspellings. Naked knuckles! Yes, it was risible, it was shameful, but I was at an age, don't forget, at which one is as obsessed with sex as infants are with sweets. Any hint of friction, of the merest physical contact, with a youthful male body, whether it was sitting in a packed bus with a standing passenger's jean-clad crotch at face-level or in the infernally hot upper circle at the Opéra, hip by hip and thigh by thigh with a voluptuously sweaty cutie-pie who didn't suspect a thing, would cause my cock to behave like Dr Strangelove's Führer-hailing arm: no matter how innocent the brush with desirable flesh, it would raise an instant and uncontrollable Nazi salute.

In school, though, such tanked-up sexual energy could prove embarrassing if you weren't too careful about disguising the appeal any one student might have for you. Roll-call was the rule at the beginning of every class and, naturally, it was only after two or three weeks had elapsed that I'd be capable of properly identifying each of my students by his or her own name. Except, just as naturally, for the sole good-looker. *His* name was as quickly imprinted on my memory as his face on my eyes, with the result that, during those first days, when I requested the class to take turns reading aloud from the Berlitz textbook, I'd find myself pointing at one nameless face after another with a necessarily impersonal 'Would *you* read?' and '*You*?' and '*You*?', till my eyes finally alit on the class's Adonis and I'd unthinkingly blurt out, '*Didier*, if you please?' Then it was back to the impassive impersonality of '*You*?' again.

I was long insensitive to the effect of so evident a bias, and it was not till one evening when I must have done it yet again, and the 'Didier' in question (or 'Patrick' or 'Marc', one of those French forenames, at any rate, that rightfully belong only to youth) not simply blushed but, aware of having been made, through no initiative of his own, the cynosure of his classmates' smirks, actually glared up at me, that I realised to my dismay how obvious had been the motive behind my favouritism, and how unwelcome my attentions, even if Didier himself were, as I knew he wasn't – Didiers very seldom are – gay.

(When I told Schuyler what had happened, he wagged a finger at me and said, 'Ixnay, Gideon, ixnay.')

Coincidentally, or perhaps not, it tended to be the attractive ones who came out with the kind of amusing solecisms which, like an adoring parent whose tot has just said the *funniest* thing, I'd rush back into the common room to repeat. There was the sloe-eyed young Moroccan, with lashes *out to here*, who, when I asked him what he was wearing, answered 'a pair of yellow blue-jeans'; and the Robert Redford-lookalike of a lawyer who, on my chiding him for arriving a quarter-of-an-hour late for class, protested that he'd been caught in 'a traffic marmalade'. I myself would get a kick out of exploiting the potential for translingual innuendo of a handful of elementary English words and turns of phrase. I particularly enjoyed teaching the noun 'bite', for example, expressing my apparently authentic bafflement at the collective spasm of blushful *sourires* and *fous rires* whenever I chalked it up on the blackboard. I knew perfectly well that 'bite' was French for 'prick' and I could easily have prepared my students for its introduction into the lesson by proposing that we all be grown-up and knowing and sophisticated about it in advance. Yet I never tired of provoking not only the gasp that the word itself drew forth from the class but also the ensuing delight taken by it in my, as they all supposed, charming, disarming ignorance of its scurrilous connotation in their own language. (I write 'they all', but the only reaction I cared about, naturally, was Didier's, Didier's or Patrick's or Marc's.)

I recall one 'Didier'. His name was actually Martial, and he was the double of Sal Mineo in *Rebel Without a Cause*, having the moistest and sultriest incisive fossa I ever saw off a cinema screen. (The incisive fossa is that short vertical furrow, the face's navel, as it were, that divides the nose from the monogrammatic M of the upper lip.) One afternoon, to my secret joy, Martial hung back after class and, as I was getting ready to leave, bashfully approached my desk. What he wanted to know, he said, was the meaning of the expression 'dire straits'. If it had been anybody else, I'd have seen off both him and his query as cursorily as was consistent with the Berlitz regulation that, however inconsiderate the paying customers might be, the staff remain at all times impeccably patient. With Martial, by contrast, given how much such a mini-tutorial would eat into my free time, I was conscientious well beyond the call of duty. I started with the expression's basic dictionary definition, supplemented that with a variety of examples, mostly in relation to financial hardships, then got him to match these examples with a few of his own. It all took about twenty minutes, twenty minutes I could have spent relaxing in the common room, but it was worth it just to be able to gaze into his orchidaceous little face with its limpid, perplexed eyes and winningly furrowed forehead. And when I asked him at the last why he'd sought this information, and he replied with a flush of embarrassment that it was because his 'favourite group' was Dire Straits, and I understood that all those well-chosen examples of mine had been for him utterly beside the point, it mattered not a whit. I had drunk him in to what was then for me the full. He was now fodder for my fantasies.

Such were my days. And my nights? I wrote earlier of the terraced café on the boulevard des Italiens – it occupied the ground floor of the Berlitz building itself – where I would have a coffee with a cigarette after my last class, between eight and nine o'clock in the evening, and where I met, without realising that she was one of my own colleagues, Consuelo whatever-it-was. I wrote, too, that I meant, later in my story, to elaborate on why I would select that spot in particular.

The fact is that its location, especially in summer, when I'd take a pavement table, enabled me to see, and be seen by, other teachers leaving the school. Why was it so important to be seen? Simply, I repeat, that in those early weeks (could it actually have been months?), I had no friends, close or otherwise, none, none at all, nowhere to go in the evening, nowhere, except back to the Voltaire. I had, I admit, plucked up the courage to buy, in W. H. Smith's wood-panelled bookshop-cum-tearoom in the rue de Rivoli, a French-language copy of the same *Spartacus* guide I mentioned before and now knew the names and addresses of the more reputable Parisian gay clubs. But after circling the *Nuage* for an hour one evening, watching from the shadows on the far side of the street a sleek parade of svelte young men swanning up in a flutter of falsettos, I felt just too scruffily English to risk entering any such club on my own. I couldn't face being even politely spurned. I needed to be taken, the first time at least. Friendly as my colleagues were, though, the instant their classes were over, they were swallowed up in their (I imagined) incident-packed private lives. Left thus to my own devices – but what devices? – I grew more and more desperate for companionship (an only child, I started to think of myself as an only adult); and by making myself so prominent on the café terrace in question, my hope was that a colleague, quitting the Berlitz later than I had, would notice me, would stop to share a couple of minutes of good-humoured banter about our respective students, then decide, why not, to order an *express* for himself and eventually, over that *express*, suggest we dine together.

It paid off. Not always, but often enough for me to persevere. I would be sitting there nursing a coffee, struggling with *France-Soir*, struggling, too, to resist watching the Berlitz exit, its 'stage door', as we called it, too intently, lest

I be caught in the act of doing precisely what I *was* doing – looking for somebody to talk to – when I'd suddenly hear a sound for sore ears, a voice I recognised, Fereydoun's or Mick's or Peter's.

'You still here?' Ferey – let's say it was Ferey – would ask.

I'd glance up, *so* surprised to find him standing over me. 'Oh – *hello!*'

'Just can't bear to leave, can you?'

'Hardly,' I'd laugh. 'I was dying for a real coffee, not the mud we have to drink at school.'

Now for the decisive moment. Would he say, 'Yeah, well, okay then. See you tomorrow,' and be on his way? Or would he indicate the empty seat opposite mine and ask, 'Mind if I join you?'

Mind if I join you? Sometimes, if it *was* Ferey, whose tendency was always to apologise for imaginary rather than real slights, I'd hear him add, tentatively, 'But maybe you want to be alone? Tell me if you do.' Dear Lord, has anybody ever been as misunderstood as I?

If Ferey did join me, it was only, as I knew all too well, because he himself had no date, nothing lined up for the evening, a humiliation – I mean not his but mine, in so abjectly praying for him to be dateless – I rejoiced in (even if it pained me), as making it all the likelier that after our coffee we'd go on to have a meal together.

Generally, we'd dine at either one of two restaurants in Montmartre, Drouot and Chartier, familiar to all Berlitz teachers, students, labourers, pensioners, the unemployed and anybody else in quest of a cheap, nourishing meal.

Cavernous hangars both of them were (and still are), with shuffling waiters like living caricatures by Sem or Forain and big-haired, bosomy cashiers flaunting their blowsy barmaidenly charms – *les belles caissières*, as Colette identified the species, each with a face like a breast on which somebody has scribbled a face. In fact, Chartier and Drouot were so exactly alike that, were you led to one of them blindfold, it would be impossible, once inside, to work out which of the two you were in. Most of their habitués were rancid old codgers (in establishments of this kind it's the clientele not the food that's greasy) who took forever to inspect the unchanging menu, one they must have known by heart; then, without fail, would order a *steak frites* followed, also without fail, by a *petit camembert*. Whereupon, to our amusement, they'd make just as much of a meal over ordering the wine, only to request, at the end of all these lengthy, picky deliberations, a *pichet de rouge*.

If there were no such thing as happiness, the world would be a happier place. As I now look back on that period, I have to acknowledge that I was happy up to a point. I wasn't poor but – it was Schuyler who explained the distinction to me – broke, a very different category when you're young and healthy and everything still seems possible. I lived in Paris, a city I'd always dreamt of living in. (I liked to say I was a francophile even in France.) Above all, I flattered myself that for the first time in my life I was part of a 'set'. How at school I'd longed to belong to a set! Now I did, and the idea so tickled me that I'd gaze at other sets, at other groups of friends, strangers to me, whom I'd study while they huddled and cuddled in cafés and restaurants and cinema queues, and I'd wonder how they could bear to go through life without knowing, missing or envying me and my own friends. (Does this make sense?)

There was, however, a however. (There's always a however.) I was not, as the French put it, 'at ease in my skin'. Yes, I told myself, I *was* happy, reasonably happy. But, as Pascal said, the heart has its reasons of which reason itself knows nothing. Not just the heart, I discovered, but the cock.

Consider one boy I did go to bed with, somebody I met not at any of the gay clubs I lucklessly frequented but in front of the Drugstore Saint-Germain-des-Prés, a notorious haunt of rent boys. In fact, it was because I stupidly took him for a pro on the lookout for a trick that it was I who made the first, maladroit but unambiguous move.

He was magnificent, a slim-hipped thoroughbred with ripe, pouty lips, fiery brown eyes and a long swanlike neck that would expand when he lost his temper (which he later did with me). He was also beautifully dressed and, even if, by hovering as close as he did to the lineup of male whores outside the Drugstore, he seemed to be inviting one to misinterpret his motive for being there, I must have been nuts to imagine that so precious and poised a creature, so clearly *de bonne famille*, could have been on the game.

Though I had just received my Berlitz salary and was ready to pay whatever it took to satisfy a fantasy, one which nearly caused me to ejaculate there and then into my grey flannels, of commanding him to sit bare-bottomed on my face, I hadn't actually gone so far as to bring up the subject of money when I realised it was only just dawning on him what I'd taken him for. Yet for a reason I still haven't fathomed, unless he'd decided on a whim to be amused instead of outraged by such an insulting *faux pas*, and even if I knew as well as he did that I wasn't in his league (I noticed him archly giving me the once-over as we spoke, as though he himself found it difficult to believe he was about to descend so low), he ended by inviting me back to his place.

He lived nearby, in a modern apartment block in the rue de Buci. I followed him along a corridor carpeted in spongy deep pile, waited silently behind him while he unlocked his front door, then followed him again through a parquet-floored hallway into the salon. It had ceiling-high bookshelves on two of its walls, as well as one of those sliding ladders for plucking volumes off the top shelf; a baby grand piano; a beige, L-shaped sofa; a wilted potted plant gasping for air near the closed window; and, in front of the sofa, a coffee table on whose transparent glass top sat a vase of white tulips, a French-language paperback copy of Manuel Puig's *Betrayed by Rita Hayworth* and two framed snapshots. One was of a clean-cut, bare-chested youth, eyes squinting into the sunlight, posed against a misty lake-and-mountain setting (even though the photograph cut him off in mid-torso, it was somehow possible to tell that his nudity didn't extend beyond the waist); and the other, peeking over its shoulder, was of my companion himself standing sulkily alongside an expressionless Andy Warhol.

Yves-Marie – he told me his name on the way to the apartment because I asked him, but when, after about twenty seconds of silence, he asked me in turn what mine was, I had the impression it was purely for form's sake – marched straight into the bedroom, then into its en-suite bathroom. He switched the light on, turned his back to me, unzipped his flies, pulled his penis out and, one hand on an insolent hip, peed into the toilet bowl. Without any visible wriggling of his buttocks – I mean, without his making any effort to shake off the odd stubborn droplet – he came back into the bedroom, his now half-erect, uncircumcised, balaclava-sporting cock poking out of his open flies in a way that couldn't help reminding me of Mapplethorpe's black model (except that Yves-Marie was neither wearing polyester nor was as phenomenally hung). Then he cast himself backward on to the bed, pulling his trousers and sky-blue underpants down to his thighs and drawing his darker blue shirt-front up over his hairless chest as far as his nipples, which left his penis free to fall back on to his abdomen, just as Gary's had, lying there as though it were scotch-taped to his pubic hair.

I omitted to mention that he had a lisp, one he made no attempt to disguise. Quite the reverse: he appeared to seek out those words and phrases calculated to call attention to what he patently saw as a quaint, upper-crust imperfection singling him out from the crowd. 'Je voudrais,' he said to me in a sleepy voice, 'que tu me thuthe.' Or, in English, 'I'd like you to thuck me off.'

I had to strain to keep my own cock from getting too excited too soon, as the last thing I wanted was a replay of earlier incidents, one of which I've recounted here. I realised too that, even if I'd had it done to me, I myself had never given a blow job in my life. And though I knew there were boys for whom inexperience in a sexual partner was unimportant, even added to his charm, I also knew that Yves-Marie was not such a boy.

I walked over to the bed and, after a moment or two of hesitation, clasped his penis by its roots. Obviously I was a bit too rough: his whole body gave a violent twitch and, without opening his eyes, he cried out, 'Mais fais atten-thion! Tu vas la cather!' ('Careful! You'll break it!') Bending over him, still trying to keep my own penis under control, yet already wise to a faint moistening on my thigh that warned me I was slowly starting to ooze out of the right nostril of my underpants, I lifted up his hot, top-heavy member; but instead of letting it gradually slide into my mouth I stuck it in all at once.

That, I could tell, wasn't the way to do it. I started to gag on this pulsating barrel-shaped tube and, almost choking, brought my teeth down hard around it. I could actually feel the serration of my lower front teeth scratch its veiny underside.

Eyes now wide open, Yves-Marie shrieked. I withdrew as swiftly as I could; but when his penis slid back out of my mouth, it was still along the ridge of my front teeth, so that he didn't stop shrieking until it was right outside. Ashy-faced, he held the bruised thing up with both hands and, gingerly twisting it over to one side, bracing himself just to look, he peered at it to find out whether or not it was bleeding. It wasn't, thank God. But even from where I stood, right at the end of the bed, I could see how inflamed was its circuitry of vertical veins.

'Ath-hole!' he spat at me in English; then, aware of the ridiculous pose he was striking, he edged himself off the bed with his underpants still at half-mast and his trousers curling round his ankles.

I myself was humiliatingly detumescent. I don't just mean my cock, which was now less a phallic symbol than, as Yves-Marie might have said, a phallic thimble. My whole body, my very soul, had shrivelled, and I could only repeat, 'Sorry. I'm sorry. I'm sorry. Je suis très, très désolé.'

He looked at me with loathing. And then he said it.

'Toi, tu ne vas jamais plaire.'

Toi, tu ne vas jamais plaire. Not 'You aren't my type', but the terrifying 'You'll never be anybody's type.'

And before waddling back into the bathroom and slamming its door on me, he added, 'T'es vraiment pas theck-thy, tu thais. Et puis – et puis t'es thale!'

I went white. This was the worst yet. This would keep me awake nights. This I'd never, never be able to joke about. I wasn't anybody's type. I wasn't sexy. And I was dirty.

When I got back into my room at the Voltaire, I threw off my clothes and examined myself in the mirror above the washbasin. I even drew my one little upright chair over to the basin and stood on it to inspect myself below the waist. I sniffed my armpits, sniffed the soles of my feet and between the toes, lay flat on the bed and, pulling my two legs right up over my head, managed to sniff not only my genitalia but (or just about) my rectum. I satisfied myself that I was clean, though I was still troubled by the fact that my hotel room had no private bathroom – whenever I wanted to take a bath, I had to ring downstairs to have a maid unlock the communal bathroom along the corridor – and that I bathed only three times a week, not every day as I'd done at home. There was absolutely nothing I could do about that, since each bath added a few extra francs to my monthly bill and I couldn't afford the luxury, but I vowed that from that day on, and every day, I'd wash myself thoroughly, all over, in cold water if need be, at the basin.

So calling me dirty was, I decided, nothing but malice on Yves-Marie's part. Was I sexy, though? Wath I theckthy? Physically, I was no John Travolta. But who is? (Not even Travolta himself, I suspected, in real life.) And, anyway, sexiness is predicated on more than just a pretty face and a wiry, jivy, hippy body. It's a *je ne sais quoi* which is in reality a *je sais très bien quoi*. You know it when you see it. And when I gazed at myself in that washbasin mirror, like the wicked Queen in the fairy-tale, I didn't see it.

I wasn't looking for love – love could wait – I was looking for action. But my sexual clock was ticking away, and each miserable misfire of an encounter so drained me of the already paltry confidence I possessed, it guaranteed that the succeeding encounter, whatever form it took, would be even more humiliating. So it proved. I may not have smelled (did I, though?), but I exuded failure, that I did know. As time passed, and my lack of experience and expertise grew all the more flagrant, my gaucheness, that gaucheness that can be so endearing in some gormlessly grinning seventeen-year-old game for anything, became more and more of an embarrassment to me. I told myself that if two gay men in their twenties go to bed with one another, then each will expect the other to know how to suck a cock without either scratching it or vomiting over it, know how to stop himself ejaculating before his partner has got himself erect, know what 'bagpiping' is, and a 'daisychain', and a 'dirty Sanchez'. I didn't. They could have been the newest dance crazes for all I knew about them. I continued to be as unsure of what was expected of me as I'd once been with my 'girlfriend' Carla (except that then I'd had the excuse of being myself as inverted as those commas). And on the rare occasions when I did get myself picked up and taken back to some young guy's apartment, and after he stripped off and opened a bedside drawer to remove a jar of vaseline, I would see something suddenly die in his face as he understood that he'd saddled himself with that dullest of sexual playmates, a not-so-very-youthful amateur. I might have transformed this drawback – my ignorance of the codes and practices of consensual gay sex – into an asset by playing the seasoned heterosexual interested to know at first hand how the other half screwed. Deflowering a straight man was, I knew, a potent turn-on for many a homosexual. But, once more, I was just too ingenuous at the time to deploy such a tactic – and I began to have the same conviction that I long believed my mother had had, the conviction that absolutely everybody but me was having fun, fun, fun, fucking fucking fun.

*

It may be a strange thing to say, given how single-mindedly I've been focusing on my penile anxieties, but I wouldn't want anybody to be left with the impression that I was the kind of gay man who, as the *gai monde* itself puts it, *thinks with his cock*. I went to the movies like everybody else, generally to the same movies as everybody else. I went to exhibitions, concerts, even the opera whenever I could afford it. I read all manner of writers, almost none of them homosexual. In fact, I have an aversion to those solipsistically self-absorbed gays, and heaven knows they exist, who are content to let their lives be not only coloured but conditioned by their sexual tastes. (For most people, a penis is something attached to a man; for the type of homosexual I'm talking about, a man is just something attached to a penis.)

I soon had an opportunity to air that aversion, for chance willed it that I was the only one of our set to dismiss as worthless trash a graphic porn movie, made in Germany, which we all went to see, Frank Ripploh's *Taxi Zum Klo*. It was less the characters' sexual shenanigans that revolted me – pissing into each other's mouths, etc. – than the fact that, between these bouts of urinary love-making, the only books they read were gay-themed novels, the only films they saw hardcore gay porn, the only television they watched softcore gay porn. I thought Ripploh's portrayal of homosexuality crass and claustrophobic and I argued the case one day with Mick, Ferey and Schuyler, who had all fallen for his tacky candour.

Mick, typically, just didn't get what I was going on about, but why should he have, since he so slavishly identified with the hero's life-style? How often had we heard him describe his ritual preparations for an evening of sadomasochism – the self-administered enema as the obligatory prelude to being fistfucked, the insertion of the cock ring, the whole pseudo-satanic paraphernalia of chain-swathed black leather? Ferey, sweet, reasonable Ferey, made the point that the movie was valuable if it helped fascinated straights to understand that being homosexual meant more than preferring sexual partners of one's own gender, a point I countered by suggesting that in my experience – in my experience? – straights, when not actually hostile, were usually indifferent to or merely bored by gay self-trumpeting. Finally, after listening to the three of us without offering a word in support of any of our positions, Schuyler remarked that, in his view, 'Being homosexual is like having red hair. It's not something you asked for or can do anything about.'

'If being homosexual is like having red hair,' I said – and I was aware, when I spoke, of my voice sounding abnormally shrill – 'then why do you all keep talking about it? Red-haired men don't endlessly go on and on about the colour of their hair. They don't make a beeline for movies starring other red-haired men. They don't parade the streets telling the whole world they're glad to be red-haired. They know that nobody else has any interest in the colour of their hair just as nobody else has any interest in the nature of our sexuality.'

This blasphemous little tirade of mine caused even the non-English-speaking members of staff who'd been talking among themselves at the far end of the table to interrupt their conversations and turn their attention to me, and I realised at once they'd made up their minds as to what lay behind my outburst. Where there's no smoke, I could see them all thinking, there's no fire.

The first to break the silence was Schuyler.

'I used to know a red-haired guy,' he said, 'and, boy, did he go on about the colour of his hair.'

Then it was Mick's turn.

'Tsk, tsk,' he said. 'Poor little Gideon's in a state because he ain't getting any.'

I wanted to slap his big fat stupid mug.

'Is that all you can come up with? "Poor little Gideon – he's not getting any!" Just because I don't come in here every morning and bend everybody's ear back with how I fucked some beautiful boy the night before till his eyes were popping out of his head!'

I stuck my face right up to Mick's and imitated his own tired old impression – one we'd all heard a hundred times – of some oafishly inarticulate gay man. '"Bootiful boy! Bootiful boy!" How come they're always "bootiful boys"?' I shook my head as though I'd gone speechless with impotent fury, but I was aware of only giving away more than I meant to of my true feelings of jealousy and frustration.

'My dears,' said Mick, running a hand through his stringy hair, 'will you listen to her. I do believe I touched a nerve. Methinks the lady doth protest too much.' (Mick also had that odious queeny trait of feminising masculine nouns and pronouns.)

'You methink –' I started to reply, and already racing through my brain was the recollection of nights spent with

Mick in clubs and bars and the possibility that he might have caught sight of me wandering aimlessly about, glass in hand, my wallflower's solitude spotlighted by some disco floor's cheesy glitterball, '– you *may think* what you like,' I corrected myself, 'but you really know fuck all about me. What is it you're saying? That I never have sex? That I'm a virgin?'

He laughed a gravelly laugh. 'Does the Pope shit in the woods?'

'What?' I replied indignantly. 'That *is* what you think?'

'Listen, darling,' he said, lighting up one of his poncy Rameses cigarettes and vacuuming the smoke into his throat, only instantly to exhale it, like a conjuror, through his nostrils, 'why don't *you* tell us what you are? We promise not to be shocked.'

Schuyler imperturbably masticated his invisible gum and Ferey alone seemed sincerely unhappy for me, probably hoping the Berlitz bell would ring, obliging us all to take up our textbooks and make for our classes. The others, English speakers and not alike, made no pretence at hiding their curiosity.

The bell did ring eight minutes later, but eight minutes were enough for me, more than enough, to insert my foot in the trap.

It was true that every morning these colleagues of mine, the Scheherazades of a thousand and one night stands, would swagger into the common room, yawning, rubbing bloodshot eyes, boasting of sexual encounters (never not successful) that had kept them up to all hours – and none of them, you can bet your socks on it, ever wearied of making a lip-smacking pun on that preposition 'up'. It was true that I was being gradually driven crazy by these accounts which left little to the listener's imagination (to *my* imagination), accounts of how they stalked their prey, took it home and fucked it silly, accounts punctuated by questions from the others whom the presence of the Berlitz's few straights seldom encouraged to temper their language – 'So, tell us, don't be shy, how big was he?' somebody would ask, and 'Was he cut or uncut?', and 'Did his balls hang low or did they stay all tight and puckered-up under his prick?' It was true that, even if I knew better than to believe every one of them, the overall result was like a game of Liar – some of these anglers' tales were untrue or grossly exaggerated, of that I was sure, but I had no way of knowing which of them were, so that, had I arbitrarily pooh-poohed any single one, I'd most likely have got it wrong. It was true that, even after months had elapsed, I had just sat listening to stories of their exploits without ever having come out with any of my own. And it was true, finally, that only now, only when Mick had started taunting me, did I realise how much I must have seemed the odd man out; or, rather, how it must have struck them that, even if I never for a moment sought to pretend that I wasn't gay, I clearly either felt sheepishly self-conscious about talking of my adventures or else – and this was far the more obvious inference – I had no adventures worth talking about.

I had to assume, too, still in the instant before I answered Mick, that they had all been gossiping about me in my absence (just as, when I was present, we gossiped about those who weren't) and they had probably already come to the conclusion that my main or even only sexual release was masturbation, that closed circuit of mind, hand and cock. Masturbation in itself carried no stigma for them. It was the subject of as much ribald common-room chat as any of the more boastworthy sexual practices. Giving yourself a hand job was a good and necessary thing, ran the argument, because you can't always be dining out. But if they were to have learned that I masturbated not, say, once or twice a week but every day of my life and that even my few abortive pick-ups would most often end with my returning alone to the Voltaire, at once scrambling out of my clothes and jerking off to the fantasy of what *I would have done* to the boy whom I had just left – who had just left me – had our evening panned out differently, they would have been disgusted. Yes, disgusted. For there doesn't exist an active, 'healthy' gay man who wouldn't find disgusting the notion of a boyfriend-less loner whacking his unappetising meat night after night in a spartan hotel room.

Everybody, I repeat, was looking at me. I had to do something, I had to say something, anything, at once. I looked back at them all in turn. Then, with greater ease than I could have imagined would have been possible for me, slipping into a worldly 'Well, if you really must know . . .' tone of voice, I embarked on a juicy morning-after autopsy of my night of hot physical passion.

Since all of this happened only days after my misadventure with Yves-Marie, I used that as a template – for my description of the boy I was claiming to have slept with that night I borrowed Yves-Marie's Cocteauesque profile and coltish physique as well as the exact shape and size of his privates – combining it with circumstantial details from whichever earlier pick-ups of mine I could recall at short notice and co-opting for my climax the most lascivious of my fantasies.

The very first thing I was asked, as I should have known I'd be asked, was the boy's name. Forced to improvise, to think on my feet, I was actually about to say 'Yves-Marie'. Then, realising that it wasn't impossible, in the cramped topography of Paris's gay scene, that one of my colleagues might himself eventually pick up Yves-Marie, I managed to come to an abrupt halt at 'Yves' with a loud mental screeching of brakes but without crashing through the roadblock of the hyphen. Naturally, the choice of that particular name immediately elicited from my audience calls of 'Gideon, Gideon, tell us all about Yves!' And so I did.

It was a good story, well told, and I seriously doubt that any of my listeners were capable of spotting the joins – which is to say, working out where reality ended and fantasy began. I related how 'Yves' and I had gone back to his place; how I'd let him strip me off and how I'd then stripped him off; how we'd showered and soaped together; how he'd taken my erect cock in his hand and, wrapping it round his own, masturbated the two of us at once; and how, so divine was the sensation, I'd had to struggle not to come too soon. (On the occasion of the real-life incident which had inspired this little conceit, I *had* come, which of course had brought the proceedings to an end just as they were getting going.) Then, I said, we lay down on his bed together and, 'Yves' now being rock hard, I let him take me in the ass until I ejaculated over his sheets – not that he minded, I added, since he was ejaculating simultaneously inside me. And then, like an alarm clock waking me out of a wet dream, the bell rang for our next class.

After a few seconds when nobody said a word, Mick swung his bag over his shoulder. I saw that, whatever he'd once thought of me, he was impressed now. He grinned.

'Well, well, well, Gideon,' he said, as we started walking side by side along the corridor. 'After all the favours I've done you, I'll expect an introduction to this stallion.'

Since, for an obvious reason, there was no question of my ever agreeing to that, I hurriedly answered, 'No fear. I know what would happen then' (meaning, flatteringly to him: what chance would I have if Yves clapped eyes on you?). 'This one I'm keeping to myself. He's got what I look for in a boy.'

'I don't have to look for it, honey,' I heard Schuyler drawl behind me, before overtaking the two of us on his way to his own class. 'I know where it is.'

We all three laughed.

But how can I communicate what that simple four-word sentence meant for me? We all three laughed, we all three laughed together, we all three laughed as equals. I was, by virtue of a small white (or whitish) lie, one of them at last.

The incident inaugurated a new era of my life at the Berlitz, of my life altogether. Something had been

63

unblocked. I felt as a motorist does when, just as he's given up hope of ever seeing space and light again, the monstrous articulated truck in the shadow of whose wall-like rear end he's had to crawl for miles and miles suddenly turns off the highway. Nor was it only my public image, my self-presentation, that had changed. The sex got better too. Not that it came close to matching my dreams (not a bad thing in a way, with the kinky cast *they* had acquired of late), but the fact that I'd been accepted into the gay freemasonry of the common room persuaded me that I was giving off less of my habitual air of hopelessness whenever I tried my luck in a club, even on my own.

Sometimes, of course, a Monday-morning *cafard* would settle on the company and nobody was up to talking about anything, sex included. Mick, Ferey and I would listlessly prepare for our first classes of the day. Schuyler, who'd been teaching so long he knew the Berlitz Method inside out, would silently train his half-moons on the *Herald Tribune* crossword. And Ralph Macavoy would sit at a corner of the table picking his teeth with the soggy edge of a metro ticket, then get up and amble out of the room, giving, as he went, a lackadaisical tug at the seat of his trousers, dislodging underpants that had got stuck fast, as I craved to be, in the crack of his backside. ('Mr Sandman, bring me a dream . . .')

Sometimes, too, most times in fact, it would be somebody else's turn. I recall Ferey, who at least had the grace to lower his voice when getting down to the nitty-gritty, telling us about a middle-aged stranger whom he'd noticed in a cinema queue on the boulevard Saint-Michel, a man who'd then sat himself beside him in an empty row in what was already a half-empty auditorium – the film was Peter Brook's *Lord of the Flies* – and who'd kept disconcertingly turning sideways to peer into his, Ferey's, face in the darkness until, something of a Lord of the Flies himself, he'd unzipped his trousers, taken Ferey's compliant hand in his own and slipped it into his (as Ferey was startled to discover) underpant-less crotch.

And then it would be my turn. Then I too would slump on to a chair, my legs spreadeagled beneath the common-room table, as though I'd been undone by an all-night fucking session. And on those days, like a masturbator whose fantasies, untrammelled by the curbs and constraints of the real world, become progressively more extreme, I found myself telling tales bearing less and less relation not just to what I did in life – and, at last, I repeat, I *was* starting to have the odd fling – but even to what I would have dreamt of doing had I been a totally free agent.

I wrote earlier of three occasions on which, a gaffe-prone newcomer to 'abroad', I made an ass of myself before adjusting to my expatriate self-image. I'd like here to relate a further two: these, by contrast, obliged me to assume, publicly, the identity of a gay man not just glad to be gay but – and this stage of a sentimental education represents the second closet, almost as important as the first, from which every homosexual must freely and voluntarily emerge – glad for the world to know I was gay.

One night at the Voltaire, well after twelve, an intolerable jungle-rock racket rose up from the room directly under mine and, preferring not to get entangled with the Tunisian porter, I decided to make my complaint in person. A dressing-gown thrown over my pyjamas, I quickly ran downstairs and hammered on the door – hammered on it because nobody inside would otherwise have heard me knocking above the cacophony that had jerked me out of sleep and then, spitting mad, out of bed. After a long moment when the music continued at the same volume as before and I started gearing up to pound the door again, it ceased as abruptly as though a bandleader had just waved an impatient baton over his musicians' heads. A moment after that, the door opened and standing in front of me was a tall, blonde, hard-faced – what Mick would have called 'fucky-faced' – girl in her early twenties, naked.

Seemingly unfussed by her nudity, that face of hers no more animated than a lava lamp, she began making excuses in an Australian twang and I could see, behind her, another, button-breasted girl, also blonde, also naked, seated cross-legged on one of the room's twin beds, her head bent so far forward I wondered whether, for a reason related to some internal 'woman's trouble' I didn't care to know about, she was trying to peer inside her own vagina.

After her apologies, the girl who had opened the door to me (her room-mate paid no attention whatever to either of us) said, with a prefabricated coyness she must have thought irresistibly coquettish, 'We're having a sort of party. Why don't you join us?'

'Join you?' I replied with a snarl. '*Join you?* I'd like to tear you apart!'

Ah! how I chuckled inwardly as I watched her deflate before my very eyes on hearing me turn the invitation down flat. No, my pretty, I thought, there are some of us you'll never have! There are some of us who have no desire to paw those awful, pushy Toblerone tits or take a bite out of that damp little apple core of a cunt!

The second incident was a far less trifling affair. Ferey, Ralph Macavoy and I decided to pay a visit to a newly opened gay club located right on the boulevard Saint-Germain and named, in English, *The 400 Blow Jobs*. It was a gangrenously hot Saturday night; the boulevard, a gaudy neon necklace of boutiques, restaurants and cafés, was jammed with pedestrians; and when we arrived at the club's front door we found a queue snaking halfway back to the place de l'Odéon. If we hoped to get in, we would not only have to stand in that queue, for who knew how long, in the company of leather boys, clones, queens and transvestites, but also allow ourselves to be ridiculed by a parade of straight male passers-by, who would (we could already see them at it) disengage themselves from their tittering girlfriends and, hands on hips, mince past us with squeals of 'Ooh la la!' and 'Regarde les tantes!' and even 'Sales pédés!'

At first, I confess, I was all for giving up on *The 400 Blow Jobs* and settling for some less fashionable joint where we'd get in at once without having to submit to any such baptism of fire. When I proposed as much, and Ferey agreed to my proposal, Ralph, my darling Ralphie, stared coldly at me and said, 'So – you're ashamed to be what you are, are you? Well, I'm not. See you both Monday.' And, without another word, he strode away from us to take his place at the end of the queue.

It was true. I *had* been ashamed to be what I was; and now I was all the more ashamed of my shame. I turned to Ferey, who didn't know what he ought to be thinking or doing, I clasped him by the arm and frogmarched us both over to the queue. It took us twenty-five minutes to be admitted, twenty-five long minutes of taunts and jeers and insults – but what unforgettably proud minutes they were for me!

So my life settled into its routine, its parallel beaten tracks, its twin ruts. There was my private life (more private than I would have wished); and there was my public life, by which I mean the eroticised re-creation of that private life thanks to which I had been able to ingratiate myself with my Berlitz colleagues.

Everything I didn't do in reality, I did in the so-called re-telling of it – fucking, fistfucking, rimming, blow jobs, watersports, even mutual nipple-singeings with Christmas candles (and how did that little frolic pop into my head?). And I did it with every conceivable type of sexual partner, with whites, blacks, browns and Orientals, and from great big burly policemen whom I let tramp over my pasty-pale body in their hobnailed boots to only just ex-schoolboys in Lacoste polo shirts, roll-necked cashmere sweaters and spotless jeans, 'barely legal' (more to the point, 'legally bare') and about to set off for Bangladesh or Brazil on their 'gap year' (another combination of words for which I had a childish fondness).

That winter, and the following spring, passed eventfully, uneventfully. My life *was* a rut, if you like, a passionless rut, but for somebody as lonely as I'd always been a rut offered so hospitable a haven of the familiar and the taken-for-granted I was unhappy if my routine was disrupted – Ferey taking a vacation, a twenty-four-hour general strike causing the Berlitz exceptionally to close its doors, a day passing without a glimpse of Ralph Macavoy shimmying along the corridor.

In the wider scheme of things my personal preoccupations were, I grant, minor, except that everybody surely has the right, the kind of right Americans call 'inalienable', to regard his or her own problems as serious without being reminded – as the tedious Peter, a radical but also a bit of a windbag, would never tire of reminding us – of famine in Rwanda or the Chinese oppression of Tibet. Even if my initiation into the common-room set had been founded on a lie, I no longer felt I was a stowaway in the world. I was amazed to discover the effect that the reinvention of my public persona had had on my emotional equilibrium, on the retreats and recesses of my psyche. I was calmer. I faced life's little snags and discouragements with relative good humour. I had no more thoughts of returning to Oxford or throwing myself into the Seine off the pont Alexandre III, as I'd had after the Yves-Marie fiasco. I was no longer prey to that phobia of phobias: the fear of anybody *who isn't me*.

What have I retained from the period? Mostly odds and ends, of no especial memorability in themselves but which have nevertheless taken root as memories will, whether 'worthy' of retrospection or not. Watching *Don Giovanni* from so high up in the Opéra gods I felt I had only to lift up my arm to touch the Chagall ceiling. Listening in rapture to Ralph talk of his unending quest for 'the perfect shirt', as one might say – as he did say – 'the perfect boy' (which he himself was for me). Laughing at a brand new recruit to the common room, a Brit, young, earnest, bespectacled, not attractive, who suddenly said, apropos of some conversational tidbit of Hollywood dirt served up by Schuyler via the *Tribune* which he, the new recruit, had overheard, 'Excuse me, Zsa Zsa who?' Managing to read *A la recherche du temps perdu* from start to finish – it took me five months, in English of course – and realising that if Proust comes up in conversation and somebody automatically mentions 'the little madeleine' you can be sure he's never read him. Dining at Drouot and Chartier. Ejaculating alone *chez moi*, without manual assistance, while reading a newspaper article on hair-raising hazing rituals at Charlottesville U, South Virginia. And of course teaching, an activity I continued to enjoy, except that, as each new class replaced a previous class, as each new set of faces duplicated a previous, near-identical set of faces, I began to have the queasy feeling only I was growing older while my students all somehow stayed the same age.

Then one day it happened.

I remember the day if not the exact date. It came at the long-awaited tag end of winter and when I'd left for work that morning the trees lining the quai Voltaire were still stripped down to their own angular skeletons. It had snowed some, but nearly all the ground snow had been washed away by overnight rainfall, leaving only the odd stray patch on the kerbside like a glob of unwiped shaving cream under the earlobe. Then, in mid-afternoon, when we least expected it, the sun had come out and, by the time my classes were over, the air had begun to feel unseasonably and unreasonably warm.

That evening the judicious ambush I had been laying in the café downstairs paid off handsomely. Schuyler was the first to appear and, instead of at once rushing off along the boulevard as he invariably would, he greeted me and without a word, without even silently nodding at one of the seats opposite mine, as though to query whether I minded if he took it, sat down. And just five minutes after him, before the waiter had brought him his kir, Ferey and Mick, having fallen in together while leaving the school, joined up with us for what Mick, who'd once spent a fortnight in Kenya, called a 'sundowner'.

We were all in a jocular mood, hooting with laughter at a *fait divers* in *France-Soir* that Mick read aloud about a party of deaf-mute gays who, late one Sunday night, had been flouncing up and down the avenue de l'Opéra and who, after some humourless local resident had rung up the police to complain, had all been arrested on a charge of disturbing the peace. Then, perhaps hoping to defuse the giggles that continued to erupt from one or other of us as ungovernably as burps, Schuyler proposed a game. We were to watch the passing parade on the boulevard and have fifteen minutes, no more, no less, to select one person with whom we fancied going to bed. If you chose somebody after five minutes, and then you spotted some-body far dishier after ten, it was too late to change your vote; if, contrariwise, you held off to the very last minute, you might find yourself obliged in extremis to resign yourself to the best of what was bound to be – sod's law *oblige* – a bad lot. None of us, naturally, had the least chance of going to bed with any of our choices, but it was good fun. Try it.

After ten minutes, after scores of couples had strolled past, and we were still all playing so close to our chests that none of us had yet taken the plunge (it was astound-ing to me that Paris, a city I'd always thought of as over-populated with sexy young things, could offer such slim pickings as soon as limits of time and space were imposed on it), I made the offhand remark that, say what you will, whenever you see a heterosexual couple together, nine times out of ten the girl will be prettier than the boy. There are exceptions, but they really are exceptions, I insisted. And I added, 'Let's face it. Objectively speaking – I repeat, objectively speaking – the female is, as everybody has always said, the more attractive of the two sexes.'

This brought forth from Ferey and Mick the incredulous reactions I expected it would; but before either of them could respond, Schuyler turned to me and said, 'I didn't know you swung both ways.'

'Oh, I wouldn't go that far,' I replied, wondering where the conversation was heading. 'Though I have to tell you my first love *was* a girl. And there have been others since,' I lied.

'It's an option you might want to keep open.'

'What makes you say that?' I asked him.

'Well, I'm not really sure,' he said. 'It's just that I read a strange item yesterday in the *Trib*. I don't know what it means – if it means anything – but some waiter has been fired from a fancy-schmancy restaurant in New York because he's gay. He's suing.'

'I thought *all* waiters in New York were gay.'

'Yeah, well,' said Schuyler, 'they're talking about some kind of a new cancer, you know? A gay cancer?'

'A gay cancer?' spluttered Mick. 'What the fuck is a gay cancer?'

'To be honest,' said Schuyler, 'I can't figure out exactly what's going on. But it seems like it's a cancer you only get if you're homosexual.'

'Oh please, give us a break! What a steaming pile of horseshit. Next thing you know there'll be a gay flu. Or gay gallstones.'

'I'm just telling you what I read in the paper,' said Schuyler calmly. 'Anyway,' he went on, 'I don't know why you call it horseshit. When I think of what you guys get up to with your bodies, it's kind of staggering you're all still here.'

'Schuyler?' said Mick.

'Uh huh?'

'Do us all a favour. Stick to your crossword, why don't you.'

Schuyler accepted the snub as unreproachfully as he accepted everything else life threw his way, and I must say that even if I myself had made no contribution to the exchange – which, anyway, lasted only a minute or two before we started playing the game again – I was with Mick on this one.

It was two weeks later when the subject arose again. Perhaps because of how well we'd all bonded in the café, Schuyler asked the three of us to meet an English acquaintance of his, a musical-comedy composer who was stopping over in Paris on his way back from New York, where a show he had written, a jokey adaptation of the *Odyssey*, had opened and closed off-Broadway on one and the same hideous night.

To begin with, I thought Schuyler was inviting us to a private supper in his apartment, an enticing prospect, since I'd long wondered how and where and above all with whom he lived; but as I ought to have realised, knowing him as I did, I'd pitched my expectations too high. He wasn't up to that yet. (Nor would he ever be.) We were to dine – Dutch, for we were all equally on our uppers, the musical-comedy composer included – in what Schuyler called a bottom-of-the-range Chinese restaurant in the rue de Tournon, near Saint-Sulpice.

Barrie Teasdale was the acquaintance's name, and he was a wag in, I would guess, his late fifties. He was camp, but in the word's theatrical as much as its sexual sense. He spoke in a transatlantic drawl, he said 'Puh-leeze' for 'Please', he divided the world (his world) into 'those who think Miss Liza Minnelli is the greatest and those who *know* Miss Barbra Streisand is the greatest' (*sic* – and Barrie was the sort of person who actually said 'sic'), he held his cigarette in the most affected manner I ever saw, in the middle of his hand, as though he were wearing a ring *between* his fingers, and he was so boundlessly pleased with himself I kept expecting him to blow preeningly on his fingernails and polish them on his lapels. He told one name-dropping anecdote after another, in not one of which he himself featured. But then, he was one of those individuals who are terror-stricken at the idea that, caught off-guard, they might find themselves saying something that isn't funny, something that isn't out-of-the-ordinary. Everything for Barrie was a joke, every line had to be a one-liner. It transpired, for example, that some years before he'd actually done time for having solicited what's called a 'pretty policeman', and this is how he told the tale: 'I was in London one wet Sunday afternoon and every-thing was closed' – except your mouth, was my unspoken retort – 'and I wandered into the Tate and I was looking at the Constables and I thought I'd pop down to the loo. Well, blow me if there wasn't a constable down there too!' So, yes, he was amusing, but he was also tiring (he sang for us all, along with our fellow-diners, in an excruciating Rex-Harrisonish *sprechgesang*, as though to leave us in no doubt as to why his musical flopped, its 'show-stopping' number – '*I escaped the anthropophagi/ Outstared the beastly Cyclops, I/ Saw the Acropolis/ And a metropolis or two . . .*'), and I could understand why Schuyler had elected to break the habit of a lifetime by deigning to socialise with us poor suckers after hours.

Anyhoo (to borrow one of Barrie's own pet word-tics), we left the restaurant at eleven to have our coffees on the terrace of the Flore. Mick, an old habitué of the café, had once known our waiter biblically and now exchanged with him an inoffensive double-peck on the cheek *à la française*. Barrie, still tirelessly holding forth, watched these kisses, fell silent, if all too briefly, then curtailed his current story, about the Hollywood starlet Pia Zadora – it seems that, during some glitzy charity event in Manhattan, a sort of *Night of 1000 Stars*, the emcee had bitchily remarked that, if a bomb were to drop on the theatre, it would be Zadora's big chance – to tell us another, very different one.

'Funny, that – what you and he just did,' he said to Mick.

'Funny? Why? He's a friend.'

'Oh, because of something that happened to me in New York. I always stay at the Iriquois – that's West 44th and 6th – and I have my coffee in the morning at the coffee shop there. You guys would find it a tad el-cheapo, I suppose, but it's right there in the hotel and it suits me fine. Anyhoo, this trip, on the first morning, I go down to the coffee shop and I see Louise, who's been there since forever – she's the manageress, not as young as she used to be but she was really something in her day, she had this helmet of jet-black bobbed hair, very twenties, very silent movie star – I used to call her Louise Brooklyn – anyhoo, she greets me, and I go to kiss her the way I always do – and, well, she backs off. I mean, she's polite and all, and she asks me about the show, and London, the usual stuff, but she makes it totally clear she's not about to kiss me. So I ask her what her problem is, if maybe I'd said something – though I'd arrived the night before, so God knows who I could have said it to – and she doesn't know what to say at first and then she says, then she says . . .' – here he adopted Louise's dem-deze-and-doze accent – '"Lissen, honey, don't take it personal, okay? But what with this cancer business, well, who's to know? You hear what I'm telling you? So why don't you just relax and I'll get you your coffee."' And,' he concluded, 'there you are.'

Where were we, though? A cancer affecting only homosexuals? It was a joke. Crabs, rashes, inflammations, piles, sores, hives, hepatitis, all of these – none of which I'd ever personally had – go with the territory, as they say. But cancer? How can cancer know what you did in bed? Why should it care? Since when did cancer become a *moral* disease? And whose morality? And, anyhoo, why should we give a shit about the puritanical prejudices of a bigoted American waitress in an el-cheapo coffee shop?

According to Barrie, there was talk of nothing else in the bars along Christopher Street and in a pair of Greenwich Village bookshops, both of them on Houston, in fact right next door to each other. One of them, run by the sort of prissy high-minded gays he called 'male Lesbians', traded in Vidal and Isherwood and Anaïs Nin and Edmund White and artsy-fartsy photograph albums of nudes by Horst and Halsman and slim volumes by slim poets laid out – the volumes not the poets, unfortunately (that was Barrie's joke) – on a single long display table so you could ignore them all at once. The other one, run by common-or-garden, down-to-earth faggots, peddled what most of us were really after if we were honest about it: porn and poppers. Gay men would go into the first, put on their solemnest faces and sagely nod through huddled discussions on the worsening crisis; then, before starting home, they would slip into the second and slip out again with the scummiest mags they could find.

He pattered on and on about Manhattan's clubs and saunas and bathhouses and fleapit movie theatres and of course the 'legendary' *Mineshaft*, with its meat rack, its torture chamber, its glory holes, its piss-filled tub and the sign on one of its walls – they actually had to put a sign on the wall! – advising patrons that no shitting was permitted on the premises except in the john. Golden showers yes, okay, why not, if that's what turns you on; brown showers, forget it.

At which point Mick, probably irritated at finding himself upstaged as our guide to the scene's 'underbelly', our Virgil of the gay Inferno, pointed out that Paris too once had such a club. Called, appropriately enough, *Le Manhattan* and situated, less appropriately, on the rue des Anglais, it had been closed down by the police, who, raiding it, had discovered a draughty warehouse-sized backroom squirming with stark naked men. ('Interesting, isn't it,' Schuyler interrupted, 'that there are two things you can be stark: one is naked and the other is raving mad.') But though Barrie found it depressing that Paris had become such a sexual backwater compared to New York, he had to admit that London was even worse. Nothing, he said, nothing at all was happening in London.

When Mick and I took our leave of both of them on the place Saint-Germain, I couldn't help noticing that they walked down into the metro station together, arm in arm, and it occurred to me for the first time – for nothing of the kind had been hinted at during the evening – that Schuyler might be putting Barrie up for the few nights he was staying in Paris. Could they, I wondered, be old flames?

When perceived from a certain angle, living in a city is like living indoors – like living inside a castle, entire wings of which are left uninhabited, to moulder under dust-sheets. There were 'wings' of Paris that, while I taught at the Berlitz, I never got to know. My daily existence was bounded, triangularly, by my quai Voltaire hotel room, by the school building on the boulevard des Italiens, along with the twinned Drouot and Chartier restaurants in the same vicinity, and by the 'village' (as we locals like to refer to it) of Saint-Germain-des-Prés, my prowling patch to the extent that I prowled at all. I would make the odd detour: to the boulevard Saint-Michel for a veal-and-pasta in a self-service cafeteria frequented by students; or, if I felt like indulging myself, to an expensive cinema on the Champs-Elysées; or out to the bois de Boulogne to fritter away a solitary Saturday afternoon watching the clownish campery of Brazilian transsexuals so extravagantly coiffed and hatted, powdered and primped, they would have made Carmen Miranda look like Celia Johnson. But these were only detours. I had *my* regular newsstand, *my* cafés – Old Navy, the Apollinaire, the Rhumerie – *my* shish-kebab kiosk in the Latin Quarter.

Money was a permanent problem. By the twenty-third of every month, pretty much on the dot, I had a shock when I did what I laughably called my 'books' and realised how little I had left till the twenty-eighth, which is when we were paid.

And there was another, wholly unexpected problem in my life. I would start to find myself glared at by suspicious parents whose infants (of both genders) I'd been gazing at for maybe a tiny bit too long in the street. Understand me, my interest in these tots wasn't at all erotic in nature; rather, I was discovering in myself the germ of a paternal and parental instinct. (Actually, when I think about it, I would make a terrible father but a terrific grandfather. What a pity you can't leap a generation.) How lovely it would be, I thought, as I watched these families out on some weekend excursion, how lovely to have some infant's trusting puppy-paw clutching my hand. I know how saccharine such a sentiment must look on the page, but there's nothing I can do about it. Having a child, I told myself, is the contrary of committing suicide, and suicide was an option I still hadn't altogether ruled out. More and more persuaded that, a pitifully inept homosexual up to then, I could have made a decent, loving family man, I dreamt of what my life might have been had I been born straight (or else as sexually eclectic as the turn-of-the-century romancer Pierre Loti, of whom I remember reading somewhere that 'he loved men and he loved women and, had there been a third sex, he would have loved that as well').

It's happened to most of us gays, I imagine, at one time or another. Yet when, in a confessional frame of mind, I spoke out about my frustrations, Mick's response was, ha ha, that he preferred to have *other* fathers' sons ('more variety') and Ferey's, just as predictably, except that his tastes always took me by surprise, that he preferred to have other sons' fathers.

Meanwhile, news of the gay cancer was beginning to filter through to us from Schuyler's *Trib*. From what we could gather, and the reports were still confused and contradictory, the disease had the effect of provoking the complete collapse of the immunity system (from an abuse of poppers, some claimed), which seemed to imply that you couldn't technically die of the cancer itself but, instead, of any malady from which under normal conditions that system was designed to protect you.

I recall the very first stories we heard about it, of once rampant homosexuals reverting to masturbation, even celibacy, of former *bons viveurs* turning into what you might call *bons voyeurs*. I read one frightening account in *France-Soir* (but could I believe it?) of a young gay New Yorker who had returned home from hospital, terminally ill, only to find that in his absence his landlord had changed the locks on his West Village apartment and slung his belongings – clothes, books, LPs, the lot – on to the sidewalk in a heap, a heap that children were forbidden by their parents to touch and garbage collectors refused to remove. Mick told us of a rumoured-to-be-homosexual Hollywood actor who'd been turned down for a role in a TV soap because his leading lady positively refused to let herself be kissed by him. And Ferey, on his return from a short trip back to the States for the funeral of his hundred-and-two-year-old Iranian great-aunt, related how, at the reception, when he offered to share his Pepsi with one of his own nieces, her mother, his sister-in-law, had jerked the paper cup out of the little girl's hand so violently she spilled its carbonated contents on to her black stiletto shoes.

I have to say, though, that the threat still felt airy, insubstantial and, above all, very, very far away, not just because we considered it to be solely an American problem – even if a couple of obscure African countries had latterly been mixed into the blender – but also because, as another *Trib* piece informed us, to be at risk you had to belong to one of an alliterative quartet of categories: homosexuals, haemophiliacs, heroin addicts and, of all unlikely targets to be singled out, Haitians. How, we said to ourselves, could we take seriously a disease so lunatically fixated on the letter H? Paris, at any rate, couldn't and didn't. If what was happening in the States was dutifully covered by the porn monthlies I bought for their pinups, they would also scoff at what everybody who was anybody on the local scene dismissed as just the latest, bogusly biological manifestation of Yankee homophobia.

Even so, it was an eerie time in which to be alive and horny. On the one hand, we were bombarded by sensational headlines in the national press: 'New York Fights Back While Paris Dances' (in *Le Matin de Paris*), 'Panic Grips Gays' (*Le Nouvel Observateur*), 'The Pink Plague' (*Le Parisien libéré*). On the other, in an article which caught my eye in one of my pinup mags, I read: 'Not a week passes without some titillating exposure of a disease that is said to be more virulent than gangrene and bubonic plague combined, a disease destined, or so they insist, to decimate us poor poofters. Let's just wait and see, shall we? And, while we wait, let's go on living. Fucking is dangerous? Well, what about crossing the street?' Another, lampooning a widely publicised report that the Swedes had already implemented a long-range plan to deal with the 'epidemic', proposed that so melodramatic an overreaction could be attributed to 'the Scandinavian fascination with death perceptible in the work of Strindberg and Bergman'. And a third cheerfully counselled its readers to ignore the 'imported illness' along with the Big Macs to which its author compared it. That one had a particularly arresting title: 'Sida, mon amour.' Or 'Aids, my love.'

For at last the cancer had been given its proper name. Or acronym. Aids. Or AIDS. Whichever – it stood for 'Acquired Immune Deficiency Syndrome'.

If I may digress for a minute, let me say that I personally have always preferred to write 'Aids' rather than 'AIDS'. The implication of the upper-case 'AIDS', after all, screeching at us as it does like a banner headline, is that this is definitely not a disease as others are. Once a week, for example, Mick, who continued to foster hopes of making it – but as what? – in the world of rock music, would turn up in the common room with the latest issue of *Variety*, a pretentious affectation given his chronic shiftlessness and, I was certain, lack of any talent for anything. After scanning the music section which was supposedly the main reason for his buying it, he would show us, on the obituary page, the list of mostly minor show-business personalities – orchestrators, assistant set designers, chorus boys and the like – who had all died at anxiety-inducing ages: thirty-two, twenty-four, even nineteen (a wunderkind of a Puerto Rican playwright who had only ever seen one of his plays staged). They were said to have passed on 'following a lengthy illness' – unspecified, natch – and also to have been 'survived by' parents, sisters, brothers, but never, never wives. Except that, almost every week too, it would be bluntly announced of at least one or two of them, either because they themselves had seen no shame in it or else because none of their 'survivors' had thought fit to insist on the canonic euphemism, that they had 'died of AIDS'. Well, it always seemed to me that, the moment you turned to that obituary page, the first thing to leap out at you were those four capital letters. It was almost as though the typeface itself were raising both its voice and its eyebrows in horror at the cause of death and the life-style which had been the cause of that cause – as though, whatever else the departed might have achieved in his life, he was doomed to be remembered ever after for what he had died of.

To return to those halcyon, ostensibly halcyon, days: considering the emergency it would one day become, it may be difficult to believe that during the next twelve months the gay community in Paris (in which I include our gay micro-community at the Berlitz) contrived to talk constantly and compulsively about Aids yet at the same time refused to let it inhibit its own, hard-won right to personal liberty and unaccountability. If even half their morning-after tales were to be credited, my colleagues, with a single exception, went on leading sexual lives as reckless as they always had, and I went on fibbing as recklessly about my own. Aids was a matter for concern, yes – but in Africa, where the origins of the virus had finally been traced, and in America, where the moral majority, homophobic to a man (and woman, let's not forget), had been accorded a heaven-sent excuse to turn the clock back on everything militant homosexuality had achieved since the Stonewall riots. As Mick put it, 'Straights can't abide the thought of us having it off together without being slung into the jug. So what do they do? They invent a disease just for gays!' French anti-Americanism, not all that latent at the best of times, was stoked up to foaming fever pitch by the advent of what Schuyler called 'Aparthaids' – doctors declining to attend patients, growing numbers of suicides, parents too afraid to comfort dying sons. Only in America, we gloated, with the immemorial condescension of the old world towards the new, and we truly did think (I speak of a time when next to no fatalities had been reported in France) that it was happening, if not only then primarily, in America.

Yet, even in Paris, the situation lent itself to all kinds of distortions and misinterpretations. I remember when, via one of his sugar-daddy connections, Ralph Macavoy secured for himself an invitation to the *vernissage* of a David Hockney retrospective at the Grand Palais. Next morning we asked him if he'd been presented to the great man and what his impression of him had been.

'Oh,' said Ralph, 'he's a real sweetie. I mean, he's totally unspoilt.' Then, after a moment of reflection, he added, 'I guess that's why I feel so sorry for him.'

Sorry for David Hockney?

'Because he's got Aids.'

'*Hockney has Aids?*'

'Yeah,' Ralph answered, and I would swear to it he wasn't joking. 'Really big ones. One in each ear. They say in a couple of years he'll be stone deaf.'

How we did laugh.

Except for the cranky night porter, whom I continued to shun, I was soon on first-name terms with the younger members of the Voltaire staff, who would permit me to take furtive baths without paying for them. Then there was the curmudgeonly Surrealist poet Philippe Soupault, who also lived in the hotel and who, when in one of his gregarious moods, would invite me into his room – a room filled, surreally, with dozens of empty English jam jars – to listen to his meandering and for me meaningless score-settling monologues. And the widowed Contessa – Contessa of what exactly? I never did learn – who occupied a suite on the floor beneath mine and who bankrolled her affluent, useless way of life by twice a year auctioning off a couple of the rare first editions the collection of which had been her ex-hubby's ex-hobby. Her grimy features were a waxy palimpsest of several face-lifts and, with her beringed fingers, kohl-rimmed eyes and weighty pearl or faux pearl choker, she resembled a raddled café-society harpy from a Brassaï snapshot. She was a frightful snob, haughty, irascible, antisemitic and, to be honest, not somebody I was always proud to be seen with: complaining, as she regularly did, about the noise made by guests in the suite above hers, guests who, I suspect, were simply walking to and fro as they had every right to do, she remarked to me once with a sour cackle that the only upstairs neighbour she could ever have tolerated was Anne Frank. But whenever we met, in the Voltaire bar or in a nearby restaurant, *La Frégate*, where she would insist on picking up the bill for both of us, I thought her, though spooky, inexhaustibly interesting. I found out quite by chance, for example, that, a Hollywood hopeful in the thirties, she had been one of the chorus girls roped to the wings of a snow-white aquaplane in *Flying Down to Rio*, an Astaire-Rogers musical I'd happened to catch in a small revival cinema in the rue Champollion.

What else? Like most of my colleagues I was constantly short of ready cash and would give private lessons on the sly, as our Berlitz contracts banned us from teaching anywhere but on the boulevard des Italiens. My kindliest, hardest-working pupils were a retired Hungarian couple who lived on the Champs de Mars (even after I'd been based for a couple of years in the city, the spectacle of the Eiffel Tower – my initial! – in the dead centre of their salon window always gave me a thrill: it was an edifice about which I was never to grow, as Mick affected to put it, 'bladed and jasé') and who, in the closing fifteen minutes of our twice-weekly classes, would serve me an 'English' high tea of cucumber sandwiches, scones and Dundee cake from a glamorous silver tea-service.

What else? I took myself off, by myself, to Tangiers for a week, in the forlorn hope of combining lust and wanderlust. It was raining when I arrived, raining when I departed, raining when I walked through the shabby souk, raining when I caught fleeting sight of a raincoated Paul Bowles in the town's tumbledown central square, raining when I glumly followed a trio of male 'escorts' (not all together but in the course of three consecutive afternoons) into the Hôtel Marie-Antoinette in a stinking side-street that even Tangerines avoided as too *louche* for comfort. Let them eat cock! – so I Marie-Antoinettishly told myself. But when I recall the sex I had there, on all three occasions, it might as well have been raining inside the hotel room.

What else? I was paid a visit, one hot and humid week in July, by a cousin of mine, Dennis, a teacher in a small Buckinghamshire boarding school. Ah now, I'd given a lot of thought to Dennis. In his mid-thirties, unmarried and likely to remain so, the despair of his grandchildren-craving mother, he was the type of art master who wore dubiously dark navy-blue shirts and those hand-woven ties that, no matter how meticulously they're knotted at the collar, inevitably end by dangling the wrong way round. A 'confirmed' bachelor, he took all his summer holidays, alone, in the Far East. My own suspicion – but I had no hard evidence to back it up since Dennis, for as long as I could remember, had been referred to by the rest of the family, with a comically awestruck respect for mild behavioural difference, as 'a very private person' – was that this Far East of his was confined pretty much to the likes of Manila and Bangkok. At home, where I'd only ever run into him at domestic dos, anniversaries, christenings and so forth, there was certainly no obligation on his part, a man fifteen years my senior, to open up to me, the nature of whose still raw and untested sexuality he mightn't even have divined. Yet in Paris the moment was surely propitious for each of us to come out joyfully to the other. To be fair, I never prompted him, never dropped a pin, as gays say, never once gave him either a cue or a clue. Yet, as we lunched together at the Coupole or glided down the Seine one foggy night on a fairy-lit *bateau-mouche* or talked in his hotel room for hours on end, up to one or two o'clock in the morning, till I felt like opening a window to let the stale conversation drift away, the subject seemed to hover over us, crying out to be caught on the wing. It never was. A week later Dennis departed, leaving me, even if I hadn't the slightest doubt he was homosexual, somehow none the wiser.

What else? I witnessed this scene at *Chez Francis*, the ultra-smart café in the sixteenth arrondissement once famously frequented by Giraudoux: at the terrace table next to mine a living, breathing gay centrefold in his early twenties – lush, layered blond hair, a rock-hard, hairless chest visible thanks to the fan-shaped aperture of his unbuttoned white shirt, and the kind of flawless facial features which always make me wonder what it must be like to be *behind* such a face rather than in front of it – was attempting to coax a tomboyish, indeed frankly boyish, pony-tailed girl in a red duffel coat to go to bed with him. She was at first coyly reticent, shaking her head a good deal; then she turned definitely chilly; and when at last they left, still in each other's company but, as was all too evident to me, only as far as the nearest taxi rank, I was once more confounded by the abyss that divides the heterosexual and homosexual worlds. For, let's face it, had I been in her position, the boy wouldn't have had time to finish his question before I'd have cried out, 'Oh oui! Oui! Oui! Oui! Oh *oui!*' at the prospect of spending the night love-locked to that long, angular, aromatic body whose low-slung jeans already afforded me a half-real, half-imagined glimpse of its converging abdominal declivities. Just what are these cunts holding out for?

And what else? After a series of formulaic letters in the early months, I ceased to receive any mail from home. I did, however, get an occasional telephone call from my mother, enquiring how I was, how things were, if I was enjoying my job and whether I wasn't ready to move out of the Voltaire into a flat of my own. (For her, the notion of putting up longer than two weeks in a hotel, no matter how modest its mod cons might be, and I don't think she understood how ascetic my room was, constituted an unheard-of luxury.) I never let on to her about my trip to London with Ferey and, even when I had free time, I tended to stay put in Paris, partly because I couldn't afford to give up my private lessons and partly because, though I yearned to travel, to laze under skies swept clean and cloudless by feather-duster palms, waited on hand and foot (and, with any luck, in between) by a race of accommodating 'natives', I had no one to travel with and not for a moment, after Tangiers, did I contemplate again setting off alone. In one of the last letters she sent before our correspondence, such as it had ever been, fizzled out altogether, she asked if I wouldn't like to spend a week *en famille* in Oxford – I could see the three of us in the back garden, father, mother and me, lolling sedately on striped deckchairs, a slew of Sunday supplements strewn at our feet. I wrote back by return of post to make the point that the trip from France to England was a once-in-a-lifetime undertaking and that it would be foolish of us not to wait till we had really, *really* started to miss each other. I could hardly believe that even she, who had only ever been out of the country twice, once to Majorca and once to visit in-laws in Oklahoma City, would swallow so preposterous an excuse. Yet she never protested and, as I said, corresponded with me less and less until, eventually, no longer at all.

But I wrote above that there had been one exception to the shoulder-shrugging absence of concern, save as a topic of conversation, with which the common room brushed off the no longer all that new menace. This was Fereydoun. From the start, he had been visibly affected by the macabre second-hand stories we all took guilty enjoyment in telling one another (the anecdote as antidote, if you will), and would go perceptibly pale on hearing the most horrific of them, those involving symptoms, bloated fungi, tumours like bowling balls, Arcimboldesque genitalia the size, shape and even the colour of cauliflowers and artichokes, that only farm animals had ever been known to exhibit. We all mercilessly ribbed him, but it was clear he was spooked. Just how spooked, though, I realised only when one evening he confidentially invited me, my last class finishing a quarter-of-an-hour before his, not to go home at once but to wait for him in the café downstairs.

Since it was drizzling when I got outside, I didn't take my regular seat on the terrace, the one which strategically faced the Berlitz exit; instead, I chose a quiet window table inside the café. But though it enabled me to spot Ferey the instant he emerged, it didn't seem to work both ways. For when at last he did make an appearance, striking me as suddenly very skinny and frail underneath his black bourgeois brolly, I noticed that he stood for a few seconds, nonplussed, before the empty terrace, as though he suspected that for some reason of my own I'd changed my mind about waiting for him. I was surprised – but I was also pleased – at how upset he appeared to be that I wasn't there and I let a few more moments go by before tapping loudly on the pane to let him know that I was.

He sat opposite me and ordered an Orangina. He didn't tremble or burst into tears or splash any of his Orangina when pouring it into a glass. (The one external sign of his jitteriness was his right hand's white-knuckled grip on the polo-neck top of his soda-pop bottle.) Yet there was something about him that made me wonder whether, if not at the end then clearly at the beginning of his tether, he might yet do any one of these things.

He gulped down half the Orangina. Then came the confession.

I didn't know what to make of it. He had been with a boy the night before – the 'boy', when I vulgarly enquired, turned out to have been an engineer in his late thirties, married and father-of-three, but gays, whatever their predilections, have a tendency to refer to any object of their lust short of a septuagenarian as a 'boy' – and he was in the process of being violently fucked in the ass when one of his teeth fell out.

It wasn't a front tooth – really, it must have been way at the back, as the gap wasn't at all visible when he tugged at the left corner of his mouth to show it to me – but it *was* a healthy one, he insisted, and it's true, given his penchant for dentists, he couldn't have had an unhealthy tooth in his head. It appears the engineer had been a good sport about the accident. In fact, the way Ferey told it, he was the type of brass-balled buddy-boy who would have gone off bragging about how he'd fucked some poor chump till his teeth fell out – literally. But he himself had instantly fought free of his partner's phallic clench, made a dash for the bathroom, his own prick still tinglingly erect, and thrown up into the toilet bowl.

I repeat, I didn't know what to make of it. I resisted cracking a joke, one I'd just thought of, about the tooth fairy (or tooth Ferey), since I could appreciate how traumatic the experience must have been, particularly for somebody given to making mountains out of molehills, or out of just moles, or even just molars. Instead, what I said to him was that a tooth falling out might be nothing more than that – a tooth falling out. It happens. It had happened to me (though not during sex). And, anyway, if he really was afraid it could be an early symptom of . . . what neither of us was willing to enunciate, why didn't he just go and have a thorough check-up?

It was then he said something that shocked me. Naturally, the first course of action he'd planned to take, he told me, was to consult a doctor – but scarcely a day passed when Ferey didn't think about consulting a doctor over some ailment or other. This time, though, *he was too scared*.

Ferey, the hypochondriac's hypochondriac, the invalid incarnate, the Platonic ideal of the *malade imaginaire*, too scared to consult a doctor? I couldn't believe it.

'What's the point of seeing a doctor,' he went on, 'if it's too late?'

'Listen to me, Ferey,' I said, 'your tooth fell out when you were having sex. Okay, I agree, it's not very nice, but perhaps you just had a rotten tooth and you never knew it. I mean, you do realise we all think you're a hypochondriac, don't you?' A hangdog expression on his face, he nodded. 'Well then, for Christ's sake, just do your hypochondriac thing. Go to the doctor and put your mind at rest.'

'People always say that,' he whispered fiercely, his lower lip quivering like a scolded child's. 'People always say, "Go to the doctor and put your mind at rest." You'd think nobody ever went to the doctor and had his worst fears confirmed. That happens too, you know.'

I argued with him for over an hour (which sounds like an exaggeration, but isn't) before his hypochrondriacal instincts gained the upper hand and, after one last endeavour to wriggle out of the ordeal with the proposal, swiftly shot down by me (but why? – it made perfect sense), that maybe he should see his dentist first, he agreed that nothing less than a medical examination would put an end to his misery one way or the other. But he added that, if he went, it was on condition that I accompany him. I was touched, and of course I agreed.

As we said goodbye (he had no appetite for dinner), he took my hand in his and said, 'Give it up, Gideon.'

I asked him what he was talking about.

'The heavy sex you've been doing. Leave it alone. It's dangerous. I know.'

I couldn't prevent myself from smiling at that. But the smile faded from my face when I noticed, almost invisible on the brow-line of his brilliantined hair, a rash of tiny blotches, some white as confetti, others pink like rose petals. Then we went our separate ways.

To my everlasting shame I forgot all about Ferey's appointment. His doctor, typically, proved to be a swanky GP whose clinic looked on to the parc Monceau. And, as Ferey had requested the soonest possible appointment, he'd been asked to turn up at this clinic at twenty-to-eight in the morning, exactly twenty minutes before the doctor's regular working day was due to start. Ferey had told me all that, he'd told me twice, and – even if it was with a stifled groan at the unholy hour that I'd nodded yes, I'll be there – I had agreed, I had promised to lend him my support.

But I forgot. On the day of Ferey's appointment I awoke at the same hour I usually did; and, my first class scheduled at noon, took myself off to *Le Divan*, the Gallimard bookstore on the place Saint-Germain, not even to buy a book but to ogle one of the store's assistants, an auburn-haired honeybun of eyeball-distending sex appeal. And it wasn't until halfway through the afternoon, smack in the middle of one of my classes, that I recalled at last what it was I'd had to do that dawn. I recalled, too, at the same instant, that I hadn't seen Ferey in school all day.

When he didn't surface the next day either, I started to

hear, inside my head, a faint whisper of alarm. I told myself at first that my anxieties about his health were just as hypochondriacal as his own. There existed lots of legitimate reasons for any teacher's temporary absence from the school. Colleagues came, went, even occasionally came again; and though one had to assume that somebody in their lives was *au courant* of the logic behind all these comings and goings, it was seldom anybody in the common room. I would have rung him up had I known his number, but we'd never got so far in our friendship as to exchange *coordinées*. And I'd have gone to see him that evening if only I could have remembered the name and number of the Right Bank street – rue Marigot? rue Mérigeau? 21? 31? – in which his apartment, one I'd visited just the once, a year before, was located. I could of course have made an immediate enquiry at the Berlitz's personnel department. But I was reluctant, only forty-eight hours into his absence, to take a step so 'official' it felt like calling the police. I didn't *come first* for Ferey, that was for sure – I didn't come first for anybody – and I told myself that the task of finding out what the matter was lay with the person or persons unknown to me, if any, who did.

On the third day, however, Ferey still having made no reappearance, I did go to Personnel, where I learned from a preppy, bow-tied young man, who already had to look up poor Ferey's name in one of the ledgers to remind himself who I was referring to, that he had left. Left the Berlitz. Resigned. The very day of his check-up. Without giving notice or claiming what meagre back pay there was owing him.

I was devastated. I had a dreadful vision of Ferey, a hypochondriac hearing at last the news towards which he had undoubtedly persuaded himself his whole life had been converging, stepping out into the air and the sun and nobody there to reassure him that things weren't as bad as they seemed. At that moment I resolved to find out what had become of him, and I asked Mick to help me. Somewhat to my mean-spirited surprise, he instantly agreed. But first of all, the preppy young man in Personnel refusing to pass on to us the information we sought, we had to figure out for ourselves where Ferey lived.

On the sole occasion I'd been to his apartment I had carefully followed his instructions as to how to reach it. But what were they? The first stage, anyway, I hadn't forgotten – take the metro to Bastille. Once there, I recognised the broad, windswept avenue I'd walked along on emerging from the metro station a year before; and even though, as I suddenly recalled, Ferey had laughed at me for taking what, it turned out, was the long way round, I decided that Mick and I should take it again and trust that my dormant memory of that initial visit would enable me to tick off each landmark as I encountered it. That, at least, was the plan. Except that it was an extremely long avenue and I was starting to fear we'd taken a wrong turning, or else missed the right turning, when I spotted an old-fangled bicycle-repair shop which I seemed to recollect (a dozen men's bikes strung up vertically side by side in the window like a row of can-can dancers); then a corner café whose *menu de dégustation*, taped to its glass door, had been tarted up with painting-by-number illustrations of its

97

stale specialities (*choucroute, omelette aux fines herbes*, that sort of thing); then, running parallel to the avenue on which we ourselves were walking, an equally long but much narrower street: the rue de la Folie-Méricourt. We were there.

Tracking down Ferey's apartment building was not a problem. In spite of the fact that its number was neither 21 nor 31 but 10, being in the street itself was all I needed to have it come back to me. We climbed the three flights of stairs I'd climbed before and I rang Ferey's bell.

I can't say now what it was I expected to see when he opened the door, but I was even more struck than before by his physical frailty, his mousy weeness. He was also blotchier. And above all, when he spoke, which he didn't do for quite a few seconds, he was a little bit breathier – a fact that made me realise that, in the three months or so prior to our conversation in the café, I had already detected in his voice, but obviously not known I had detected, an almost inaudible wheeze that would punctuate the blank spaces between his spoken sentences.

Since the curtains were drawn, the apartment was in pitch darkness – why? – and Ferey had to fiddle for some time with an inconveniently positioned bedside lamp before bathing the three of us in a creepy blue light. This was carried out in silence. He had motioned us in, but he hadn't said hello or expressed what would surely have been understandable astonishment at our presence at his front door. As he tried to locate the lamp-switch in the dark, the only remark he did make – and he was somebody I couldn't recall ever having used a four-letter word

– was 'Why's the fucking thing never on the same side as your fucking finger?'

'Ferey,' I said after a moment, 'I'm sorry, I'm really sorry.'

'That's all right,' he answered dully, and I was unsure if he understood what it was I was apologising for.

'I mean I'm sorry I didn't go to the doctor with you. It's not as though I had a good excuse. I didn't. So I'm really sorry.'

'It's okay. Forget it.'

There was a short silence. Then Mick, bursting with an impatience in which his compassion for a friend in distress battled, as I could tell, with his prurient curiosity as to what precisely was the matter with him, asked him straight out what was going on, why he had resigned from the Berlitz, what the doctor had told him.

Ferey had Aids.

Not that he'd been diagnosed with Aids. He hadn't yet been diagnosed with anything. But he 'knew' he had Aids.

It appears his consultation at the parc Monceau hadn't even lasted half the twenty minutes allotted it and had consisted altogether of an unaggressive probe of the back of his throat with a glinting instrument resembling a pocket-sized shaving mirror. After which examination, the doctor had scrubbed his hands, sat down behind his desk, started to write up his report and, while still writing it, told Ferey he had some kind of yeast infection on his gums. Then he asked him, virtually in an aside ('an articulate cough' was Ferey's description), if he was a homosexual. Ferey had replied no. Gazing at him over the rims of his spectacles for so long Ferey was convinced he was offering him a second go at the question, the doctor eventually referred him to a colleague of his, an eminent immunologist at the Hôpital Cochin.

When I heard that, I felt something shiver inside me. We were all now aware of the Cochin's reputation as the centre of French research into Aids.

Ferey also informed us that, at the Cochin (to which he'd gone straight from the clinic), when he'd glanced round the waiting room before his turn was called, he'd recognised a podgy, curly-haired man pacing to and fro, fro and to, who though he was in reality no longer podgy except in his lower abdomen where, whenever he sat down, an unmistakable colostomy bag would cause his lap to balloon up like a double-page spread in a pop-up book, and though, as well, the tide was ebbing on the once opulent mane, was nevertheless the same podgy, curly-haired estate agent he had been fucked by several nights in a row five months before. It was quite a coincidence, except that, with Aids, there were no coincidences.

It was unthinkable now for either Mick or myself, after listening to Ferey, to try and persuade him that he was only being his old hypochondriacal self; after, too, I'd gone into his lavatory and observed, smearing the bowl's inner rim, a not so very small star-shaped blob of blood-streaked shit. Oddly, it wasn't so much the blood as the shit that disturbed me. I'd never used Ferey's loo before but, had I given the matter any thought, I'd have assumed it must be as cloyingly hygienic, even when no visitors were expected, as he himself always was.

He'd already had a biopsy, a sliver of his gum had been

removed and he was waiting for the results. But he also told us – calmly – that if he *was* calm it was because there was no suspense to be on tenterhooks about. He absolutely knew what the tests would show. As for the Berlitz, well, there were those spots breeding on his face and that wheeze that both Mick and I could hear plainly enough.

'So what are you going to do now?' Mick asked him.

'What do you think I'm going to do?' Ferey said. 'I'm going to die.'

Aplomb wasn't his forte, however. He wasn't Schuyler. Immediately after saying what he did, he soundlessly slithered to the floor and, before either of us had time to make a move in his direction, he began to scream, so loudly we both jumped.

'I'm twenty-four!' he screamed up at us. 'I'm twenty-four! I'm fucking twenty-four!'

For a few seconds I stupidly stood there, listening to him scream, not knowing how to handle him, which end to pick him up by. Then Mick pushed me out of his way with a snort of 'Oh, really!', gently lifted Ferey off the carpet by his armpits, sat him on the sofa, sat down beside him, laid his head on his own shoulder and stroked him like a dog while he sobbed. He himself said nothing. He just cradled and hugged Ferey, all the while disentangling strands of un-brilliantined hair from his damp forehead.

It was about half an hour later when Mick and I left the apartment, Ferey having composed himself sufficiently to ask us to go. ('Yes please. Yes, I'm fine. Yes, I'll be all right. I just need to be alone.') We walked back to the Bastille metro station by the same circuitous route we'd come. For a fair stretch of that miserable grey avenue neither of us said a word. Finally, I turned to Mick and told him how sincerely impressed I had been by his having found just the right way to deal with Ferey.

'You know, you're really good at it.'

'I ought to be,' he said, with a grin so wide its two ends actually seemed to jut out beyond his cheeks. 'I've been a father figure since I was twelve years old.'

We parted inside one of the corridors of the metro.

To whoever is reading me let me say that I narrated the scene above at length because, as I was even then aware that it would, so it did constitute a new turning point in my life. Even now, I still find myself thinking of that walk along the windswept avenue, of the bicycle shop, the corner café, its menu's painted *choucroute*, and the sight of Ferey's face, not yet 'ravaged', no, but already *polluted* by the illness we knew was hibernating behind it. I'd long believed that the true distinction between a serious disease and one that wasn't serious was that the former was something you yourself got and the latter was something other people got. Be honest, I'd say to myself – nobody else's disease is ever quite as serious as anything you yourself have to cope with. But that was because I'd known nobody of whom I could have said that his affliction *had also become mine*. For the first time in my life (not, I know, the first time I've committed that phrase to print), I understood what it meant to suffer, to mourn, for another as for myself. And I realised that this – 'solidarity', I guess, is the word for it – that this solidarity could be traced to the fact that Ferey, dear to me as he was but not personally more than that, was gay and I was gay and he had Aids and gays had Aids and his condition (homosexuality *or* Aids) was my condition, however different our tastes, however different our 'difference'.

In any case, that was the very last time I ever saw him. In his apartment, while Mick was cradling and comforting him, I myself had at least had the presence of mind to make a mental note of his telephone number and, in the weeks following our visit, I regularly rang him up. Nearly as regularly, though, my calls went unanswered, to the point where, more than once, I wondered whether he might have packed up and returned to the States. (What I did know was that he wasn't an in-patient at the Cochin, as, despairing one day of ever being able to re-establish contact, I actually phoned the hospital and asked – in vain, to my relief – to be put through to him.) Then, when I was about to give up altogether, he unexpectedly would answer. We'd talk, but non-committally. When I enquired how he was, I was naturally thinking of his health above all. But I tiptoed around the essential and that's how he chose to respond. 'Oh, not too bad,' he'd say. Or 'As well as you'd expect.' Never more than that. Even when I suggested our spending an evening together, his reply was never a categorical yes or no. 'Oh, sure. Sure. We've got to get together. Maybe have dinner at Chartier. I'll call you.' I gave him the Voltaire's number, but he didn't call.

For me, there was to be one unforeseen consequence of Ferey's departure, and that was my own belated *rapproche-*

ment with Mick. Obsessed as I'd always been with our set – Schuyler, Ferey, Mick, myself and, more marginally, Ralph Macavoy – I'd forgotten the constancy with which the Berlitz's cast of supporting characters would replenish itself every five or six months. The gap opened up by Ferey's absence, the offstage rumble of tumbrils, the introspective silences that had begun to mark even our most humdrum exchanges – though we all continued to brag about our sexual exploits, real or imagined, our hearts were less and less in it – suddenly made me realise that I was now surrounded by faces which were as familiar to me as those I'd been exposed to when I arrived at the school but which belonged to lately appointed teachers whom I hadn't bothered getting to know, so content was I with my own clannish little clique. Without quite noticing it had happened, I'd become one of the doyen's cronies – I was shocked to overhear a recent recruit refer casually to 'that old fart Schuyler' – and new sets had meanwhile formed which prided themselves on being just as exclusive as ours. There was something else, too, which went beyond these petty intramural rivalries. Because of the spread of Aids the whole atmosphere in the common room had changed. The high spirits, the *joie de vivre*, the jazz and pizzazz, dash and panache, that even now I would claim were inherent properties of homosexuality, and properties that had been for me, considering my woeful track record, almost more important than the physical ones, had evaporated. Since the quotient of homosexuals on the teaching staff was visibly (and audibly) as high as it had ever been, the collective mood and morale could scarcely avoid reflecting in miniature that of the gay world at large. The gay world? Gays weren't any longer very gay.

More than ever, I needed somebody I could turn to, somebody I could talk to. Schuyler was Schuyler, a human tautology. As for Ralph Macavoy, he had only ever flitted over the surface of my existence. So there was no one else but Mick – Mick who had conducted himself gracefully and affectingly during that awful night at Ferey's and who, despite what I still thought of as his phoniness, turned out to possess a sweeter nature than he'd probably have wanted anybody to guess at.

The funny thing about Mick was that, even if the specialised nature of his own 'proclivities' – his word, not mine – must have struck him as having put his life more at risk than most, he had always been the most stridently vocal of any of us about the attitudes and platitudes, the crises and hypocrisies, of the Aids discourse, about what he insisted was the covert homophobia of anybody, gay and straight alike, expert or layman, who had attempted to sound the alarm. I can still hear him arguing in that sometimes grating drawl of his about how spurious were the risks we had all allegedly started to run. 'Jesus, Schuyler, don't tell me you're so fucking naive as to swallow that?' he would ask across the table more than once, when in truth, on the Parisian gay scene, reluctant as it had initially been to face facts, support groups had at last been set up and Samaritan telephone lines organised. For the longest time he refused to budge. When Schuyler ran his forefinger down the obituary page of Mick's own copy of *Variety*, snapping it whenever he noted a 'following a lengthy illness . . .' or a 'survived by his parents . . .', he, Mick, would exclaim, 'Can't you get it through your thick skull that that kind of euphemism doesn't reduce panic – it aggravates it?' He once came up with a rather good *mot* on the subject, if one that had long since been overtaken by events. He proposed that the only gays who had cause to worry were those who already had 'angst in their pants'.

Even Mick, though, finally got the picture, and it was then he and I started to see more of one another. He would invite me, if his last class ended ten or fifteen minutes after mine, to order a coffee for myself in the downstairs café so that we could afterwards go on to dinner together. For much of the time he was still the same salacious Mick of old. He still delighted in provoking me, over a *steak frites* and a *pichet de rouge* at Drouot, by complacently cataloguing the extensive gamut of his kinks and quirks. He told me, for example, that as a little boy he had secretly enjoyed pissing in his underpants and now, a big boy, it was other men's underpants he liked to piss into. 'Urination will be my ruination,' he joked – *not*, I suspect, off the cuff – and we both knew it was a joke he could make only because, of all the sexual high jinks he got up to, that one was among the less dangerous.

But we also gradually began to have more serious conversations, often late at night on the terrace of the Flore. Divesting himself of his campy mannerisms as abruptly as a quick-change artist, he would speak to me of his efforts to carve out an entrepreneurial pop-music career for himself modelled on that of his hero Malcolm McLaren (who, it seems, was unforgivably condescending to him the one and only time they met), of his coke addiction and subsequent detox, of the unbroken sequence of failures that had dogged him since his late teens, when he had apparently (this I could believe) edited a magazine at his public school so brilliantly provocative even his headmaster, who had been horrified by the publication in it of some vaguely homoerotic drawings of the sexiest sixth-form boys, predicted – wryly, I suppose the word has to be – that Mick would go far. But he hadn't. He hadn't gone anywhere. He'd achieved nothing of what he'd planned to do with his life, not even – he allowed himself the ghost of a smile – managing to put an end to it. (He wouldn't elaborate.) I liked him at last.

One night, after a session at the Flore, Mick asked me whether I'd care to accompany him to a *partouze*, an orgy, to be held in some luxuriously large apartment on the rue du Bac whose joint proprietors were a Lacanian psychoanalyst in his forties and his much younger, privately wealthy lover, an Argentinian. I instantly agreed, even if it was amazing to me that there were still such things as orgies. I was also troubled by how rigorous its etiquette would be. Mick impressed on me that whoever, during the night to come, I found groping me, or sucking me, or fucking me, or, maybe worst of all, kissing me, I was prohibited from rejecting even the most unsavoury of comers. If I agreed to go, I'd also have to agree to shed all my sexual hang-ups, all my personal tastes and distastes, along with my clothes.

It happened to be his own first visit to the apartment

(the fact that he wasn't personally acquainted with either of its owners seemed not to matter); but though we had no problem getting into the building, he had mislaid the scrap of paper on which he had scrawled the specific number we were looking for. So we wandered up and down a grandly curving, lushly carpeted and totally deserted staircase that slowly revolved around us as in a dream or a film, all five storeys of it, and we were actually about to call the whole thing off when, on the fourth floor, I heard him shout 'Aha!' behind me. I turned. He was bent double over one of the landing's three green household doors. He pointed something out to me. I too bent double and saw, taped to the door at no more than an inch above floor level, a square white card on which was written, in the teeny-weeniest of block capitals, 'OUI, C'EST ICI.'

Mick had to ring the bell several times before a vertical crack opened up in the doorway, a crack in which one of our hosts, if that's who he was, was just visible. He was forty-fivish and had the curdled allure of a prewar matinée idol; his gleaming mouthful of teeth was underlined – more precisely, overlined – by a pencil-fine moustache; and, over a menorah-shaped bush of silver-grey chest-hair whose wispy upper branches circumnavigated his nipples prior to heading for the navel and points south, he wore a yellow terry-cloth robe bespattered by what resembled bullet holes but which were probably cigarette burns. He looked first at Mick then at me and waited for one of us to speak.

'Je suis l'ami de Serge,' said Mick.

'Ça va,' said the other; then, without a further word, he

opened the door and let us in. We stepped inside and silently walked behind him along a narrow hallway. On either side of us, on the pale-papered walls, was an identical row of evenly interspaced oblong patches where paintings of monetary or sentimental value or both had been unhooked to be safely stowed away for the duration of the *partouze*. Halfway along the hallway, the door to a bedroom stood ajar.

'Laissez vos vêtements là,' we were told. 'On est dans le salon.' And indicating another door that lay directly ahead, negligently knotting the cord of his robe about what we were now aware was his head-to-toe nakedness, he took his laconic leave of us.

Though the drawing-room door was closed – before reaching it, our host had taken a right turning, maybe into a kitchen or bathroom – I identified the music we could hear from beyond it. It was an old hit song, 'The Little White Cloud That Cried', by Johnnie Ray, a sometime crooner or bobbysoxer, whatever the word was, of the sub-Sinatran school, famous for being deaf (he wore a conspicuous hearing-aid on stage) and, I fancy, long since deceased. If I knew both him and his hit, it was in part because he'd been one of my mother's favourites and in part because, as a boy, I'd been told by cousins Lex and Rex, while we were all sifting through mother's record collection for just one album we could bear to listen to, that he'd once been arrested for soliciting in a public loo in Detroit or Duluth. I recall thinking it strange that Ray should be a solicitor (like my own father) as well as a singer, even stranger that he would choose a lavatory to conduct his business in, but I couldn't see why it deserved to be considered a criminal offence.

Anyhoo, Mick and I entered the bedroom, whose canopied bed was already heaped high with male underclothing and overclothing, and proceeded to undress. We started by stripping down to our indoor clothes. But that, naturally, was just the beginning. Instead of our stopping there, as though we were then about to go, arms linked, into dinner, off came our shirts, socks, shoes, trousers and finally – I cannot convey how unbelievably perverse this felt – our underpants, until we stood buck naked in front of one another.

'You okay?' Mick said to me.

I nodded, nervously game.

'Allons-y.'

As we started walking towards the salon, I got it into my head that when Mick opened the door everybody inside would instantly take time out from what he was doing to size us up and mentally determine which of the two of us was the more fuckable. (I was better-looking, I thought, but there could be no argument as to who was better-hung.) Well, not for the first time, I was wrong. When he did open the door, and the closing bars of Ray's dirge blasted out at us, louder than life – *'he told me he was very lonesome/ And no one cared if he lived or died/ The little white cloud that sat right down and cri-eeeeed!'* – nobody looked up, nobody at all.

'Pity we didn't keep out clothes on,' I murmured to Mick. 'We might have got more attention.'

What met our own eyes, meanwhile, was almost indescribable. There must have been a good two dozen men in that room, the majority of them, hooked up to each other via every conceivable type of conjugation and copulation, stretched out on the floor. But two guys were squatting on the salon's sole remaining armchair, one of them fellating the other, the servicer's head, like one of those tactically and tactfully stationed vases of sunflowers or ping-pong bats by which genitalia used to be obscured in naturist magazines, masking what I could only suppose, since I couldn't see it, was the servicee's tumescent cock. There were a trio of overweight men squeezed on to a divan almost as wide as it was long, but (maybe just as well) it was impossible to work out what they were up to. And there were yet another four, younger and fitter, thank God, performing a hip-grinding conga around the edges of the room – by now, the music had switched to a jolly, jazzy polka by, I think, Nino Rota – each of them, like elephants trunk-to-tail in a circus parade, clasping the cock in front of him by an arm extended through the furry underpass of its owner's buttocks.

I noticed, too, pushed back into a corner, a bamboo coffee table on which, next to what was presumably somebody's gift to our hosts of a Barbie doll still in its miniature cellophane coffin (sequinned evening gown, blonde candy-floss hair, formal elbow-length black gloves), three small bowls had been placed side by side. In the first was a dry white powder; in the second, poppers; and in the third – which, visibly, had had few takers – condoms.

Waved at from across the room, Mick left me after a few moments to greet a friend – Serge, I supposed – who was sitting on the floor, legs splayed, with someone else's legs, one to the left, one to the right, dangling over his two shoulders, this same someone else's feet cradled in his hands. As soon as Mick joined him, they sank out of my sight into the gyring and gimbling roomful of slithy toves.

Now alone in the doorway, seemingly of no interest to anybody, I felt more exposed – the word may appear an ill-chosen one under the circumstances but it's the only word – than I'd ever been in my life. A tide of memories swept over me of early, solitary excursions to clubs and bars in London, when I'd had to pretend to be the wilful loner I was trying so hard not to be: memories, though, which were as nothing compared to the nightmarish reality of my present plight. I was, after all, not only alone but stark naked, the stuff of nightmares indeed, the more so as I couldn't shake off the impression that I was the sole naked guest at some fashionable, fully-clothed cocktail party. (I actually found myself cupping the palms of my hands over my crotch 'to cover my shame'.) What to do? Even at conventional get-togethers I'd never been blessed with the kind of suavity that allows one to insert oneself into some self-sufficient little circle of strangers whose conversation, in full swing, one casually interrupts to introduce oneself. So how in God's name, taking to a whole new level a socialising skill I already didn't possess, could I be expected to approach somebody I didn't know from Adam and, without even preparing the ground with the small talk of foreplay, start sucking him off? That, I knew, was the way it should be done, the way it had to be done if it were to be done at all – nobody else, it was evident, was about to take the initiative – but I just couldn't bring myself to make the first move. Moreover, my solidarity with the condition of homosexuality in its every manifestation, even the most kinkily extreme (nothing gay, to paraphrase the philosopher, was alien to me), had just been put to the severest test – by *that conga* – and failed it. There was something so ugly and demeaning in the sight of those gay gargoyles, those dancing, prancing, mincing, naked grown men ('Grown men!' – that was what my father would sneer when the rest of the family used to settle down to watch on TV the weekly cavortings of Benny Hill and his stooges), that I was, I admit, for the first time since my evening at *The 400 Blow Jobs*, ashamed to be gay. Ashamed to be what I was. Ashamed to be seen with such loathsome freaks. And when I realised that my cock had become as much of a shrinking violet as I myself was – I had to tug at it like a recalcitrant shirt-front to keep it a presentable length – I knew I wouldn't be able to stay in that house a second longer.

Without alerting Mick, I darted back into the bedroom, quickly dressed – as I was the first to leave, my clothes were still top of the heap – and quietly let myself out.

After Ferey the second of my gay acquaintances to depart the common room, a few months later, was Chris Streeter, who, once I'd been introduced to him in my early Berlitz days, had dropped out of the circulation of my life, as he has out of this memoir of it. He was rosy-cheeked, I think I've already said, and so far as I was able to judge had the kind of pleasant, bovine personality usually associated with a spanked-bottom complexion. I'm aware of no reason why we never got to know one another better. It may have been little more than that, during my first formative weeks at the school, the schedule of his classes was out of sync with that of mine and, once the moment had passed, there was no catching up.

So I was unprepared for the news I heard one morning from Schuyler. Chris had been – not dismissed exactly, but discreetly invited to quit when one of his students complained of having noticed a row of prominent bluish bumps on what were already abnormally reddened hands and wrists, and another student, just three days later, reported that he'd had to wind up a class halfway through because his forehead had erupted in beads of sweat and he'd even had to grasp the back of his chair to prevent himself from fainting. Both of these students (and once a precedent had been set, others were to follow suit) hated to rat on a teacher for whom they claimed they had nothing but esteem and neither of them, heroically, made mention of Aids. But the situation soon reached the stage where more and more members of his classes owned to having felt unease at handling exam papers after they'd been corrected – read 'touched' – by him.

What Schuyler couldn't tell me was whether Chris actually did have Aids and had left without offering any resistance to his summary sacking or else had been threatened with exposure to his family: when hired by the Berlitz we had all had to sign a form notifying our employers of our next of kin, and I wouldn't have put it past them to exploit such information against us were ever the need to arise.

But when I begged leave to doubt that he'd contracted a disease that, we now knew, presupposed the kind of violent sexual activity nobody could imagine him getting up to, so soft and girly had he struck us all, Schuyler revealed that Chris, in his cups, had once told him how, two or three times a year, he would fly off to some impoverished Central African country where, for a song, he would be free to satisfy and even satiate his lawless taste for seriously underage boys, for shiny little black green apples. What's more, the reason he'd left England in the first place was that he'd been caught *in flagrante* with one of his thirteen-year-old prep pupils. 'They didn't believe me when I told them we were just good friends,' he had tipsily grumbled.

It seems that Schuyler, who'd got to know Chris rather better than most of us, had been present, as always, early one morning when the latter had re-entered the school, four days after his official dismissal from it, to stuff into a TWA flight bag the few personal articles he kept in his *casier*. When he was ready to leave the common room, empty as yet except for Schuyler, Chris held out a friendly hand.

'What did you do?' I asked.

Schuyler stared at me.

'You schmuck,' he said serenely, 'I shook it.'

Ultimately, though, not even cool, unruffled Schuyler would prove immune to panic and paranoia. In the next few days I noticed how he started to resemble, so to speak, a camel in reverse. For exactly as it's said of camels that they're capable of travelling several days without water, so Schuyler now never appeared to have to go to the lavatory.

Not once thereafter did I – nor did anybody else, as I learned on exchanging notes with colleagues – find myself peeing beside him in the Berlitz's admittedly far from pristine WC. How, given his consumption of coffee, he contrived to hold it in all day I'll never know, but contrive to hold it in all day he did.

And then, another three or four months later, during which the dynamics of the common room would alter almost out of recognition – that end of the table, for example, that had long been 'reserved' for us, for Schuyler and Ferey and Mick and me, had gradually been usurped by a half-dozen unobtrusive gays, the kind who couldn't have made their wrists limp if their lives depended on it, 'straight' gays, straight in everything but their sexual orientation, buttoned-up in both the sartorial and the psychological sense – then it was the turn, inevitably, of Mick himself.

On the night he confided in me, our roles for once were reversed. It was he whose last class finished earlier than mine, and it was he who beckoned to me, when I passed it on my way home, from inside the same café on whose terrace I had so often lain in wait for somebody, anybody, to talk to. He had installed himself, moreover, at the very same window table I myself had sat at when striving to reassure poor Ferey he wasn't at death's door, and as I crossed the café floor from the entrance to his table I noticed him leering at a couple standing together at the bar – leering, rather, at one half of the couple, a superb specimen of blond, pale-skinned Aryanism, German, Austrian or Swiss, twenty or thereabouts, ridiculously fetching in finickily stitched lederhosen, his hair gorgeously blow-dried, an upturned tiara of a grin affixed to his freckled features like a smiley-face lapel badge. (The other half was a goateed middle-aged man, French, with a red woollen scarf wrapped around his neck varsity-style.) So, I thought to myself when I sat down opposite a blearier and more unshaven-looking Mick than I was used to, whatever his problems might have been – and I already had an idea what they were – at least he hadn't lost his eye for a pretty face.

Indeed, when I was about to ask what was up, he immediately shushed me to remain silent so we could both follow, as he'd already started to do before my arrival, the woo that was being pitched alongside the otherwise unoccupied bar. The middle-aged Frenchman, naturally, was doing most of the talking, and what we could hear of his pitch was straight out of a user's manual to the protocol of the gay pick-up. It was all there – the preliminary chat about everything save the matter at hand, the coy comparison of ages (the boy, Franz, was nineteen), the indulgently avuncular tut-tutting over youthful bad habits ('Tu fumes trop, tu sais'), the obligatory allusion to the sexual mores of the ancient Greeks ('Ah oui, les Grecs . . . ,' murmured Franz in his guttural French, the pfennig finally dropping) and, just when Mick and I were wondering if it was ever going to happen, the unambiguous pass.

It worked, as they say, like a charm. After about seven seconds of dutiful self-counsel, freckly Franz nodded, stubbed a half-smoked cigarette into an ashtray, bent down to insert his crumpled pack of Marlboros inside the top of one of his thick woollen stockings, just under a sexily scarred knee, then followed the dirty old frog out of the café.

Mick tipped his chair back and smiled at me.

'Couldn't have done better myself,' he said. 'I trust you listened and learned?'

'What was it you wanted to see me about?' I asked him.

We were interrupted for a moment while a waiter took my order. Then Mick, his smile as brusquely swept from his face as by a windscreen wiper (the quick-change artist again), said, 'I wanted you to be the first to know.' A brief pause. 'I've got it.'

'You've got what?'

'Jesus Christ, Gideon, what the fuck do you think I've got? Rhythm?' He lit a cigarette. 'Aids, what else. Oh, and please, don't say anything silly and' – perched in mid-air like crows on a washing line, his fingers mimicked a pair of inverted commas – 'well-meaning. It's official.'

In reality, though I didn't of course say this to him, his announcement came as little surprise to me, and all I could think of to begin with was the belief I already had that, so long as somebody like Mick had been spared, somebody who got up to what he got up to, Aids couldn't really be the plague it was said to be. Now that he had it, I knew for certain it was.

But I was to discover, too, that it was still possible to be shocked even when you weren't surprised, and it wasn't simply a matter, as it's so often been with me, of codified grief, of putting on my solemnest face, which is how

Barrie would have phrased it. I've already written that I'd initially resisted warming to Mick – basically, I suppose, he just wasn't 'my kind of person' – but I'd now known him a good while and, as somebody said, our best friends aren't those we like the best but those we've known the longest.

I was also, as at Ferey's, struck by the total absence of hysteria, of mawkishness, in the tone in which he talked of his symptoms – in particular, of the diarrhoea that he'd had for several weeks, that was making his life at the Berlitz a daily torment (his constant fear, he said, was of shitting his pants in class) and that had finally impelled him to consult the doctor who, just the day before we met, had given him the bad news. Mick, in short, who had treated endless numbers of 'bootiful boys', if he himself was to be believed, like so many wads of gum, chewing them up then spitting them out when he'd extracted all their succulence and flavour, was now able to speak to me – of what was, after all, a terminal illness – with a maturity he'd never shown in the sex life that had, precisely, brought him to this pass.

He left the Berlitz soon after but, unlike Ferey, he didn't lose contact with me. He'd ring me at the Voltaire eager for common-room gossip (of which, by this time, I could supply him with next to none), then tell me his own gossip, less of his health, about which he was uncharacteristically reticent, than of his voluntary involvement with one of the many new Aids-related bureaux and organisations. And, one day, he asked if I'd care to attend its twice-weekly gathering. I agreed and we arranged to have a drink first at the Flore, 'for old times' sake,' he said. Then, on the point of hanging up, he also said, 'Don't be too taken aback if you find I've changed.' He wouldn't reveal what he meant by that and I didn't insist. But I did prepare myself for the worst.

I couldn't, though, have got things more hopelessly wrong. The Mick I saw on the terrace of the Flore, saw with an amazement bordering on stupefaction, looked ten years younger and healthier than the one I'd always known. He'd had his hair cut off until all that remained was a smooth, even bristle that made him appear not terminally ill but terminally cool and contemporary. He'd exchanged that never too thrilling scarlet-lined cloak of his for a Bogartian trenchcoat, its rakish collar framing the shoulder-straps of a freshly laundered boiler-suit. And instead of the Rameses cigarettes he affected at the Berlitz he was smoking a cornpaper Disque Bleu. As for his complexion, it was what you might call interestingly pale. Aids, I couldn't help thinking, became him.

When I told him how much I preferred this new 'look' of his, endeavouring to sound as though I truly meant it (which I did) and were not paying him an easy, lazy compliment, he was amused that I thought his 'work clothes', as he referred to them, might have represented some sort of fashion statement. Under normal circumstances, I'd have taken such offhandedness as just another of his poses, but now I found myself believing him, especially as, with frequent glances at his wristwatch, he was clearly itching for us to get going.

I swallowed the last of my coffee, paid for both of us – Mick was unemployed, after all – and was preparing to leave when he turned to me.

'Look, Gideon,' he said calmly, 'I hope you realise you're going to be a bit of an outsider tonight.'

'An outsider?'

'Yeah.'

'I don't get you. It's for gays only, isn't it?'

'What I mean is, *you* don't have Aids.' He stared at me boldly. 'You don't, do you?'

'No, I don't.'

'Well, you'll be the only one there who doesn't. Now do you understand?'

'Let me get this right. What you're saying –'

'What I'm saying is that you'll be there as a guest, not as one of us. They're all militants, don't forget. You know the type of gay who'd only talk to other gays? Well, now the only gays some of these guys'll talk to are gays with Aids. So best not to mention you don't have it.'

This was unbelievable. Like every other homosexual, I'd had to learn how to live with exclusion from the straight majority. Now, because I still had my health, and because the pleasures of gayness had had to capitulate to the politics of what might be called Aids-ness, I was to be excluded all over again – and from my own kind!

'Things have changed, Gideon,' said Mick. 'We've found a cause – we've *become* a cause. Anybody who isn't with us is against us.'

'For Christ's sake, Mick, *I'm* with you!'

'Not if you're clean you aren't. For them' – and for you,

Mick? I wondered – 'you're an anachronism. You're irrelevant. I'm sorry, but that's the way it is. So say as little as possible, okay? In fact, just be your own sweet little self.'

'I'll positively ooze charm,' I muttered.

'Don't ooze anything,' said Mick, gathering from the tabletop a thick loose-leaf folder out of which bulged a sheaf of papers. 'Just be nice.'

The gathering was held inside a disaffected, gasometer-grim *atelier* situated in a Montparnasse street from which every trace of Bohemian local colour, assuming it had ever had any, had been expunged: the sole vestige of a shady past was an indelible sweatshop stink that subtly hung over the room. When we arrived, late despite our precautions, Mick, seemingly a born activist, at once left my side, just as at the *partouze*, to confer with his 'comrades' about the distribution of some roneotyped tracts, and I was suddenly on my own again, feeling as superfluous and conspicuous – conspicuous by my *own* absence, as it struck me – as I'd once felt at *The Scarlet Pimp*.

The attendance was a motley mix. I noticed a sleepy-eyed stumblebum who'd probably wandered in solely for the coffee and sandwiches; a half-dozen gaunt young scarecrows, three of them on crutches, all of them visibly in the last stages of their illness; a few dowdy business types, suede-gloved and paisley-scarved, who would have been more at home at some accountancy firm's annual dinner-dance, if such things are ever held in Paris; a tall, genial, handshaking, silver-templed gent in his sixties, parodically Texan, who wore a denim suit and a Stetson hat and spoke in a foghorn bass that I could still hear booming away from the far side of the room; a pair of (I assumed) ballet dancers whose scrawny *volupté* was set to advantage by the most elegant garments in the world – the tights, sweaters, vests and leggings of backstage rehearsal togs – and whose beady, greedy piglet eyes never stopped darting about them, taking the measure of anybody not too far gone to be picked up; and even, standing to one side as I was, two women, a statuesque stunner in her mid-twenties, chaste and sculptural, and (I again assumed) her wealthy, plain, not to say plug-ugly, if exquisitely mannered and manicured, sugar-mommy.

But Mick – for whom I found myself, to my bewilderment, feeling strangely happy – was right. I was an outsider, an irrelevance, even an insult, to these Aids sufferers – more so, in point of fact, than the pair of Les Girls (as male homosexuals, stressing the 's' of 'Les', like to call their female counterparts), since they at least turned out to be on close kissy-kissy terms with virtually all of those present, including Mick himself. And in a way that, as I say above, reminded me of evenings I'd spent at the *Pimp*, so here I tried hard to appear casual, at my ease, an old hand, as though I were attending the meeting for the same reason as everybody else, not because of the natural tribal sympathy any healthy gay might be expected to have for those of his fellows who had fallen victim to an incurable disease – more than one speaker from the floor insisted on the importance of practising what they all referred to as 'safe sex' (an admonition accompanied by rueful moans from the audience) – but because I too was one such victim. I tried, in short, as I realised with something approaching panic, to look *as though I myself had Aids*.

From that very evening on, I was assailed by the most fantastic of apprehensions. Night after night, sweating and sleepless, slathered in a hot-and-cold, sweet-and-sour sweat, I would turn my predicament over and over in my head. For consider: not only was I once more as isolated as I'd been before lying my way into a spurious intimacy with my fellow gays, it gradually started to dawn on me that, because I'd left Schuyler and Mick and Ralph Macavoy, all that was left of the original band, as well as any of the others at the Berlitz who had ever bothered to listen to my boasting, with the impression that I'd been leading a sexual life just as rich, raunchy and violent as theirs, why – it would eventually occur to one of them, Mick, say (it was bound to be Mick), to ask me – why didn't *I* have Aids?

The height of perversity it may seem – when what any sensible person would expect would have been for me to be above all *relieved*, relieved more than words could ever convey, that every single one of those tales of mine of being fistfucked till I was blue in the bum was merely the squalid fantasy of a haggard, hollow-eyed masturbator – but my primary concern at this stage was that I was finally going to be caught out. I saw myself, the one gay man in the world not to have Aids, the lone survivor of a veritable Pompeii of petrified lovers, shown up at last for the wretched mythomaniac that I had always been in reality. I fantasised that ailing and dying gays, repelled by my insulting good health, hence by my lack of solidarity with the cause, the only cause which any longer mattered to the homosexual community, would begin sending me white – or maybe pink – feathers through the post. I started – it's fantastic, as I say, but it's also true – I started half-wishing I might actually catch the bloody disease myself if it meant I could once again feel part of a family, part of a set. I even flirted with the folly of ringing up Mick and making the solemn but wittily worded announcement, wisecracking through my tears like a born fag, just as the simpering heroines of Victorian romances used to smile through theirs, that I *had* caught it.

Not only that. I entertained a notion that was crazier still, a notion that, had I ever had the nerve to act on it, would, I knew, have destroyed my already compromised capacity for rational thought and action. I told myself that, if I actually were to ring Mick – and he were to gather me, as he doubtless would, under his capacious father-figure wing – then there would inevitably have to arrive that moment when the 'deterioration' of my health would begin taking its irrevocable, *visible* course, and I wondered, I seriously wondered, whether I could go as far as to *make myself up* to look the part, faking a web of picturesque lesions on my face and hands!

That period of delirium proved to be of mercifully brief duration, thank God. Or thank, instead, my unbridled libido, which raged on oblivious of the dangers it would expose me to were I capable of satisfying, outside my fantasies, its increasingly intemperate appetites. For so unignorable did the risks now appear, so terminal and unconditional was the disease, admitting of so few exceptions and mitigations, so clearly had it dug in for the long haul, I soon found myself with a whole new set of apprehensions to contend with. Considering how becalmed the gay scene was becoming, considering the stories we'd all heard of promiscuous homosexuals, friends, friends of friends, or friends of friends of friends, metamorphosing overnight into paragons of monkish abstinence and chastity, I was now seized with terror at the prospect that if I didn't have my share of sex at once *I might never have it at all*.

That, I made a vow to myself, I would not, I could not, let happen. And one stifling summer night, as I lay naked on top of my bed's cool quilt, it suddenly came to me how I might turn a public calamity to my own private advantage.

Oh, this resolve of mine wasn't anything like as calculated as I make it sound. I never deliberately set my sights on emulating Don Giovanni's *mil e tre*. But if (I excitedly told myself) the blanket of fear and foreboding that had settled on the scene meant that fewer and fewer homosexuals continued to play the field, it meant equally (now I could actually feel the hairs tingle on the nape of my neck) that those who were still up for a regular fuck – for all that they had been forewarned a hundred times about the dangers of unsafe sex – had had of necessity to lower the threshold of their expectations where the quality of their partners was concerned.

From having glimpsed the odd, and not notably furtive, flirtation at Mick's meeting, which I'd seen openly exploited for its pick-up potential by more than a few of those who attended it, I knew that there still existed such homosexuals. And I was also reminded of the anecdote that Barrie Teasdale had been telling us at the Flore when he interrupted himself to watch Mick kiss his waiter friend. Remember: if a bomb were to have dropped on the *Night of 1000 Stars*, it would have been Pia Zadora's big chance. Well, it finally hit me – and I realise that the straight mind-set, should any straights be reading me, will regard as the epitome of faggoty superficiality my yoking together in this fashion a piece of showbiz trivia and a major human tragedy, but what the hell – it finally hit me that a bomb *had* dropped on the homosexual world. So why shouldn't Aids be *my* big chance?

It was in a bookstore that I met Kim. *Le Minotaure*, run by a pair of fortyish queens in the rue des Beaux-Arts, spe-cialised in movie memorabilia, 'intellectual' comic-strip albums, art-historical monographs and porny surrealist arcana, and the most prestigious of its habitués – all I mean by that is that I chanced to see him there more than once – was the director Alain Resnais. One morning, on my day off from the Berlitz, I was browsing through a pile of tat-tered old editions of the film journal *Positif*, some of them dating back to the early fifties, when I heard a feminine-sounding if nevertheless patently masculine voice put a question, or what was certainly pitched like a question, that left both owners – and me too, first time I caught it – baffled. 'Lady Putty?' was what we heard. And when the customer was invited to repeat his query, and could only say simply, blankly, 'Lady Putty, pliss?', the older of the two queens (longtime companions, I surmised) shrugged his shoulders, said in a languorous tone just this side of rudeness, 'Désolé, mais . . . ', and turned his attention back to the paperback novel he had already been reading when I entered the shop fifteen minutes before.

I still hadn't seen the customer's face. From behind, all I could tell about him was that he was short and had tufty black hair and – because he was wearing a sleeveless white teeshirt – slim, downy arms. (I dote on down.) But just as he was giving up and going, I got it. Lady Putty? Lya de Putti! He meant Lya de Putti, of course, one of those demented divas who palely haunted the silent cinema screen. Almost without realising I was doing so, I spoke her name aloud, which made the now grateful customer, half-in and half-out of the shop's front door, turn at last to beam at me. My heart melted, my cock swelled.

He was eighteen, from Seoul. He was based, however, in Tokyo, a trainee *maquilleur* for Estée Lauder, and he was in Paris for *prêt-à-porter* week. He was also (I was touched by such an outré taste in one so young) a fan of the more exotic silent movie stars, both female, Putti, Brigitte Helm, Pola Negri, and male, Valentino, Ramon Novarro, Rod La Rocque – except that, as I gathered from his very iffy command of English, he understandably preferred collecting images of them to watching their films. I observed him with fond fascination as he thumbed through the *Minotaure*'s systemless jumble of dog-eared sepia stills, from which he soon unearthed a handful for his own collection; and under the queens' now cynically amused scrutiny I helped him extract the change to pay for them from his tiny blue Smurf purse.

Kim was as lean as a whippet. If it's possible to be short and gangly, he was it. Though I knew instantly he was homosexual, he wasn't at all effeminate, even when he giggled, which was a lot. His French was nonexistent, his English not much better, so that, for the first time in my life, I was deeply grateful to the Berlitz Method. As for his facial beauty, the spectrum of sexual tastes being as inclusive as we all know it is, I really can't see the point in describing it at futile and probably counterproductive length, except to say that it was 'me'. Let the reader visualise a face for himself.

When we left the shop, I treated him to a club sandwich and a Schweppes at the Flore; and since his afternoon was to be taken up doing whatever it is *maquilleurs* do at fashion shows, we made a date to meet on the place Saint-Germain-des-Prés at nine.

I tried to kill time by going to a six o'clock screening of a film, one whose plot I found next to impossible to comprehend, distracted as I was both by my doubts as to whether Kim would keep our date and my wish-fulfilment reveries about what we'd get up to if he did.

And he did. In the cinema I'd noticed despite my itchy state that some scenes in the film I was watching, a hammy and hackneyed old Hollywood potboiler made in the nineteen-thirties, much of it set in the South Seas, had had recourse to crude back-projection. Well, as I hurried along the boulevard Saint-Germain and, from a distance, made out the diminutive Kim, standing alone in the Drugstore entrance, it felt to me, too, as though everything behind him, the Drugstore itself, the rue de Rennes, the lit-up Tour

Montparnasse, blotting out the sky like the keyboard of a giant accordion, were so much stock footage, all of it belonging to an alien and less luminous world than he who was to be the star of my evening.

Since, for the duration of *prêt-à-porter* week, Kim was obliged to share a room with another Estée Lauder employee in a Right Bank hotel, we went back to the Voltaire, foiling the night porter by stepping first into the bar for a drink and sneaking upstairs half-an-hour later through a now abandoned kitchen. I wasn't permitted to bring guests back to my room after ten in the evening and it had already occurred to me that getting him out of the hotel either at dawn or in the wee hours of night, depending on whether or not I'd risen to the occasion, might well prove to be a thornier proposition. But I told myself I would cross – or throw myself off – that bridge when I came to it.

Once inside the bedroom, whose frugality startled him, Kim asked if he could use what he charmingly called 'the roo', which I interpreted, correctly, as 'the loo'. I told him there was none in the room itself and that the nearest was a communal WC on the landing below mine. Or else, I added, my heart beating like a bongo, he could use the washbasin, as I generally did. He giggled; then at once unbuttoned his flies (rather than unzipped – 'zips not ere-gant,' as he put it), stood, his back to me, up against the porcelain basin and let the cold water run. Nothing at first seemed to happen. He giggled once again. 'Not come. Is hard in pubric,' he sighed, turning to face me with the whitest and toothiest of smiles. I no longer hesitated. I stepped up behind him, looked down at his uncircumcised cock, which, held as it was between his thumb and index finger, resembled a tiny, almond-hued balloon waiting to be inflated, and – saying to him (even though I knew he wouldn't understand what I was talking about), 'Shall I be mother?' – inserted my own thumb and finger around its base. I gave it a shake. Nothing. I shook it again, less gingerly. Still nothing. Then, with my left hand, I turned the cold tap on full blast and suddenly, glistening like morning dew, the pee came – I felt it course through his little rainpipe, through his lovely little drainpipe – causing Kim to laugh delightedly. When he'd done, he said to me, 'Liggle it.' So I liggled it – liggled it till its flaccidity started to stretch and firm in my gentle clutch.

Kim stayed in my room till two in the morning then slipped away – it seems without attracting the porter's attention, since the subject was never brought up by Madame Müller. And during all the time he was with me he just couldn't resist – like most boys of his age, gay and straight both – twiddling his cock, tugging it, fingering it as though it were a rosary or a set of worry beads. But then, what else in the world but a cock, one's own or another's, instils so instant and enduring a sensation of well-being, only by being touched? And I remember thinking: if God had not meant for boys to play with their cocks, He would not have made their arms just long enough to span the distance from shoulder to crotch. A cock is one of the wonders of the world – what am I saying, is *the* wonder of the world – and not much in that world is as iniquitous as the fact that it contains billions and billions of cocks ('billions and billions of cocks' – has there ever been so divine a conjunction of words?), all of them seen by God, that jammy bastard who sees everything, but next to none of them, alas, by me. It's all the more iniquitous in that there will surely come a time in the near or far future when, with the invention of some as yet undreamt-of radiographic technology, everybody on earth will gain at least virtual access to everybody else's private parts and look back with disbelief and pity on the benighted twentieth as a century of unimaginable sexual deprivation. I thought, as well, of a comment once made by the dissident Soviet poet Andrey Voznesensky. Speaking of certain especially reactionary members of the then Politburo, he said – and I quote from memory – that they had faces so ugly they ought to be hidden in trousers. For the period it was certainly a courageous joke to make publicly, and it was also quite witty, but, oh, what a calumny of the most mysterious object in the world. That metaphoric, metamorphic member, that dusky, musky muscle, that acorn that already harbours the embryo of a great oak, that dual-purpose contraption, so comical yet so awesome, that would be an unnameable monstrosity were it to protrude from an armpit, let's say, or a nostril, but that, just where it is, just where it's supposed to be, makes the isosceles triangle of a boy's limbs so enchanting and male nudity so much more interesting, so much less predictable, than female! (A man can mentally strip a woman, but how, with the least hope of accuracy where the bulge in his pants is concerned, can a woman mentally strip a man?) Hide God's masterpiece in trousers? If I were dictator of the world, I would make it a capital offence to hide a cock in trousers. I would make it compulsory for every boy and man on the planet, all those billions and billions and billions of them, Voznesensky included, to walk around with his cock flying in the breeze. I would –

Basta! All I meant to convey by that paean to the penis, my own penis's last stand, my libido's last hurrah, was that I could have spent the whole night just monkeying about with Kim's – which was, as I say, on the smallish side but compensated for that by being lovably chubby and kind of spouty – without feeling the need to gravitate to any heavier-duty stuff. And, indeed, because of my wonderment at his cock's dexterity – as also because of my fear that, if I proposed or attempted something more robust, I would spoil what was shaping up for me, by contrast with earlier disasters, as practically an idyll – that really is, as I remember it now, all I did do. I didn't fuck him, nor was I fucked by him. I didn't rim him, nor was I rimmed by him. I flicked my lithe lizard-tongue over his sweet, sweet *cojones* and invited him to sit his plump, olivy little buttocks astride my nose (that old fantasy of mine) while I gave him the daintiest of blow jobs. Not so dainty, though, that it didn't make me come at once over my own abdomen, which meant, as always, that I was abruptly no longer in a fit state to be given a blow job by him.

That could have been that – the usual – except that I remained throughout on so elated a 'high' (I decided, if I may be allowed a groanworthy pun, that I definitively preferred, or at least until something better came along, Asian cocks to Caucasians) it never struck me that Kim might have sought a more energetic session, particularly as he too seemed to get pleasure out of the tame adolescent games we did play, even if not as much as I did. But when – at around two, I say – he started to dress again, he looked at me sideways and said, almost word for word, what Carla had been about to say so long ago, 'You funny boy, Gideon.' When I stared back at him, not knowing whether I ought to take offence, he explained what he meant: 'You rike Bambi sex.' Then he kissed me on the lips, unlocked my bedroom door and slipped away. He was flying back to Japan the following day and I never saw him again.

Bambi sex? So was Kim, too, disappointed with me? Even just minutes after his departure, when I was already starting to review in my mind the chronology of the night's events, complete with slow-motion replays of its highlights, even then, as I mentally relived activities I couldn't imagine Bambi getting up to with Thumper, I had to acknowledge that once more I had let my partner down. And if I can't pretend that on this occasion anxiety gnawed at me as voraciously as it had so often done in the past, I did go to bed just a shade less euphoric than I expected I would. A cloud no bigger than a boy's genitalia had cast its shadow across what I'd hoped would become one of my most precious memories, and I resolved that with my very next 'conquest' I would properly lose, and not just mislay, my onerous virginity.

This next conquest was Mathias, a Swiss mathematics student, immensely tall, well over six feet, handsome in a brainy-looking way albeit not actually my type. We got talking while queueing for a film in an antiquated *cinéma d'art et essai* near the Sorbonne, we occupied adjacent seats inside the steeply raked auditorium and we went off for a drink afterwards.

He was a strange one, was Mathias, and I would have been content to forgo the sex that was clearly going to end our evening together – a prospect that was already implicit in our chat in the queue – if he himself had not been so keen. He had, though, an unnervingly ponderous presence at odds with what I could only presume was his lust for me. In the café where we had our drink, there was a permanent absence of anything approaching a smile on his face whenever I cracked a joke. And three or four times, out of the blue, he would ask, in French, a dumbfounding question whose relevance to the conversational matter at hand was moot, to put it mildly. 'Was Thomas Alva Edison a homosexual, do you suppose?' or 'Haven't I seen your face on the back of a Penguin?' (he couldn't recall the name of the writer he had mistaken me for) or 'Do you like dinosaurs?', to the last of which I could only reply, helplessly, that I could take them or leave them. He would, moreover, voice these questions without launching any of them in my specific direction so that they hovered between us like telephone calls waiting to be answered except that I wasn't a hundred percent sure they were for me.

An hour or so later, after walking along streets washed by rain that had begun to fall just as we entered the café and stopped just before we emerged from it, like a chambermaid conveniently making up your bed while you're in the hotel's breakfast room, we arrived at his *chambre de bonne* in the rue de l'Estrapade. I immediately enquired, as Kim had done, if I could use the lavatory. It turned out to be a communal one, like mine at the Voltaire, further along the same top-floor landing as his own studio; and as I started to walk back out of his room, I heard him ask, 'C'est pour chier?' ('Is it to shit?')

'Eh . . . en fait, oui,' I replied, trying not to sound too embarrassed. 'Pourquoi tu poses cette question?'

He grabbed my hand, drew it to his crotch and made me feel his stiff cock – a thing of outlandish, even Tom-of-Finlandish, proportions – under his jeans.

'Parce que je vais t'enculer. Tu comprends maintenant?' ('Because I'm going to fuck you. You understand now?')

He then held out his right hand towards me and unexpectedly stroked my chin.

'Mais comment? Tu es imberbe?'

'Imberbe?' It was a word I didn't know.

'Beardless,' he said in heavily accented English. 'You don't shave?'

I blushed. 'Twice a week. I'm blond. It takes a while to show.'

He stroked my chin once more.

'I like it,' he said, unsmiling.

The lavatory was of the hole-in-the-ground variety. Hunkered down, I started having second thoughts. I'd never been sodomised before and anticipation of being skewered by that member of his – as I imagined it, it would be a kind of hara-kiri from behind – was already causing my own cock, by the speed at which it was starting to shrink into its soft scrotal throne, to signal to me its malaise at what lay ahead for both of us. I made up my mind. Leaving the hole unsluiced – from his room Mathias would certainly have heard the sound of flushing – I slunk along the landing and down the stairs and it was only when I was about to step out into the street that I remembered the resolve I'd made to myself.

If I were to creep away now, I'd have to mark up the encounter as just the latest of my sexual indignities (even if this would have been the first time *I* had ever walked out on somebody else). No, I said to myself, the new me couldn't let that happen; and, a moment later, I closed the front door from the inside, tiptoed back upstairs and reappeared on the top-floor landing as though nothing untoward had occurred in the meantime.

Glowering at me with that unsettling intensity of his that I'd already come to fear, Mathias at once asked, 'Qu'est-ce qui t'a pris si longtemps?'

'Oh, tu sais . . . ' I replied, closing the door behind me.

There followed on his part a few seconds of silent rumination. Then he said, rather insultingly, 'En fait, c'est mieux comme ça. J'aime pas les culs sales, moi.'

He did, as promised, sodomise me. It was a methodical screw, raspy and dry, performed without any lubricating fluid, joyless to me but the way he liked it. To start with, the crack in my buttocks, far from magically sliding open as I imagined it would, instead chose that moment to slam shut, so that he had to use his swollen, scarlet but sickly grey-knobbed cock like a battering ram to shove his way inside my dark, subterranean grotto. The pain of being laid siege to brought hot, salty tears to my eyes. I tried to gasp and even to scream, yet no sound emerged, except a faint putt-putt-puttering, inaudible to the naked ear, from the depths of my throat. My face scrunched-up on the pillows of his bed, I thought when he eventually did succeed in impaling me, ramming his manhood home, right up to the hilt, *my* hilt – I thought, I say, what a schoolboy must think when choking on his first cigarette: *this is supposed to be fun?*

Yet, an hour later, when I came walking out into the street as bandy-legged as the grizzled comic relief in some old-fashioned, black-and-white western, not daring to imagine what my bare, bruised backside must look like, I knew for the first time from personal experience something I'd only ever glibly theorised about: that the essence of the homosexual act, of at least one type of homosexual act, is its very *virility*, an exacerbated virility, virility squared, cubed, veiny, bulgy and bestial, the virility of the Superman who lurks within every Clark Kent. Who lurked even within me, reader, who lurked even within me!

It was then that began my systematic exploration of everything the city had to offer the not too picky homosexual with an unhealthy mind in a healthy body. Nothing was to be too squalid for me, nothing was to be too risky, nothing too violent, too homespun, too butch, too camp, too Boschean, too Genetesque, too anything. I had a season ticket to gay sex and I was set on getting my very last pennyworth out of it.

I had spent my life, or what I had lived of it thus far,

cowering in a network of self-constructed fortresses that I had used to shield myself from the real world in which I knew I was a charlatan. I had inflated my few torpid sexual encounters into a flamboyant anthology of copulations that may have fooled my friends but had left me myself more frustrated than ever. I was now determined to enter that world, to experience those copulations at first hand – at first cock – to be pumped full of liquid love by a firing squad of partners, at least some of whom, I hoped, would have the tact to be charmed rather than dismayed by my inexperience and whose own sexual versatility and virtuosity couldn't fail, I also hoped, to add a sorely wanting lustre to my still amateurish technique.

I no longer remember with clarity the half of my many and various lovers – but, let me think, there was Victor, French, twenty-six, who had, *en ville*, the nerd's tic of poking, with his forefinger, his speckle-frame spectacles back up along the smooth bridge of the nose they would keep sliding down, but who turned out, *en privé*, to my very pleasant surprise, for he was a real slob clothes-wise, to have a beautifully proportioned, tentacular body with what felt like more than the biologically approved number of limbs, all of them as adjustable and adaptable as the appendages of a Swiss army knife. There was Drew, a twenty-two-year-old graduate student from Chicago with sandy pubes and a curlicued, comma-shaped cock, who taught me that, once got the hang of, riding a boy was as instinctive as riding a bike. I rode him bareback, like some human, hairy Harley-Davidson, at the local YMCA, where he was temporarily putting up in a cell-like room with even less furniture than mine at the Voltaire. There was Benjamin, a nervous, flighty, slightly spotty, slightly smelly adolescent whom I met, on his nineteenth birthday, during an entracte at the Opéra (double bill of Stravinsky's *Oedipus rex* and Ravel's *L'Enfant et les sortilèges*), when I watched him guzzle a whole glass of beer at a single go, his eyes swimming heavenward like those of a newborn babe drunk on its mother's breast-milk. He took me to his parents' (empty) house near the Montmartre funicular, where he disappeared at once into the bathroom and reappeared after eleven minutes. (I timed it.) When I started unbuttoning his jeans, and discovered that he was naked beneath them, he looked at me as though daring me to suspect the worst and – here he took a deep breath – said not very convincingly, 'I *never* wear underpants.' (I myself was dying for a pee when I left him an hour later but resisted asking to use the same bathroom for fear of what I might find stowed away not quite out of sight.) There was Damon, a Cuban, ageless, a political refugee, so he said, who had actually been 'rounded up' inside one of those stadiums in Havana one had heard about, so he said, and who gave me a brisk businesslike fuck with, unlike Mathias, lashings of vaseline. There was André, late thirties, a martyr to sciatica, with a Roman emperor's fringe and morosely smouldering features that were dolorous or just droopy depending on whether or not he was your type. A *triste* tryst. And there was smily Oscar, a Senegalese, twenty-one, a law student who lived in the Cité Universitaire in a cell even smaller and barer than Drew's at the Y. Blacker still than his jet-black skin – how was this possible? – were his Frida Kahlo eyebrows, his hard-as-tintacks nipples and his enormous conical prick whose roots felt as massive as those of a Californian redwood. When it was fully erect, I could barely move around his tiny room.

There was monkey-faced Barbet – claimed he was fourteen but he was fifteen if he was a day. He picked me up at the Deligny open-air baths one sunny afternoon (he was playing truant from school) after noticing how transfixed the roving handheld camerawork of my eyes had become by the precocious bulge of his wet trunks which, preceding him by a full three inches as he sashayed, the rubbery little rapscallion, along the poolside, revealed as much as it concealed of his face's roughneck relative from the wrong side of the waist. In the mildewy cubicle we shared for no more than ten minutes he instantly took charge – today the Deligny, tomorrow the world! – sitting me, all but pushing me, down on to the cold, damp bench, pulling those trunks of his to his knees and, like Bette Davis or Joan Crawford, slapping me across the cheeks – paf! paf! paf! paf! – with his lively, snaky, literally laugh-out-loud-amusing penis. There was Cleanth, a sinisterly jovial, bearishly hirsute American, twenty-nine, bushy sideburns, a horrendous scar – the result of some motorcycle accident – stretching down his woolly spine from his neck to his buttocks, who asked me if I was up to swallowing what he called, with ghoulish gusto, a 'fudgesicle'. Not sure what it was but recoiling from the sound of it, I declined. There was a myopic English-speaking, Cambridge-educated Egyptian boy, twenty, whose name I never quite caught (Suliman?

Soliman? Solomon?) and whom I permitted to give me a blow job even though he was in the snivelly throes of a bad head cold (he pronounced the word 'underpants', not altogether unjustifiably in his own case, as 'udderpants'). There was Edouard, twenty-eight, a journalist on the magazine *Gai Pied*, with long tapering fingers stained by a writer's inky stigmata and liquid brown eyes that were less obscured than set in relief by a pair of rimless glasses. Good, affectionate, conventional sex, nothing kinky, saw him three times in all. There was Achille, eighteen, a typical Left Bank moocher, who resembled Ralph Macavoy a little if I half-shut my eyes, not in the least if I didn't. 'Ah, vous autres Anglais! Quelle tristesse dans le plaisir!' he had the nerve to say after a strenuous hour-long fuck. There was Ian, a Liverpudlian, twenty-six, one of those beer-bellied compatriots of mine whose sole frame of reference is soccer, snooker and the *Sun* and who, when sober, behave as other nationalities behave only when drunk. I encountered him at the Café de la Paix, where he was having difficulty ordering a pot of Earl Grey from a bloody-minded waiter – sex satisfying enough in a brutish British way. And there was Consuelo from the Berlitz, just for the heck of it. Wilde was right. Cold mutton.

There was fey, squeaky-voiced Maud, a boy, real name Roger, twenty, very swishy, as close to being a transvestite as you can be without actually wearing a skirt, in fact sexier clothed than naked, for he had an ignoble putty-coloured prick as puny as a penny-whistle. There was Ivor, South African, middle-aged, a balding balletomane with a gorgeous Greek lover in tow. It was the lover, Yannis, nineteen, whom I naturally fancied and, after having had to put up with Ivor's insufferable chatter on the terrace of the Flore (directed to what I was privately glad to observe was a sullen and rebellious Yannis, it was all 'Tell Gideon about the perfectly lovely Peter Pears recital we went to at the Wigmore' and 'Tell Gideon who it was we saw camping it up in the interval of *La Bayadère*' and 'Tell Gideon what Peggy Ashcroft said when you asked for her autograph'), it was Yannis I finally got when he and Ivor had a fearful public row about how loud the latter was speaking. There was Gaetan, a French-Canadian airline steward, thirty-one, pretty if ravaged – the debauched choirboy look – the pockets of whose chic linen, slim-lapel jacket were filled with matchbook covers on which his many, many lovers had jotted down their telephone numbers (homosexuality, the love that dare not speak its name but doesn't mind leaving its number). I accompanied him to his room in a hotel off the boulevard Raspail, the Istria, where, beneath snapshots of Foujita, Man Ray, Marie Laurencin and the like, who had all shacked up there when it was called the Hôtel de Grenade, he fucked me so ferociously that, back at the Voltaire, I found blood-red skid marks on my underpants. There was Julien, twenty-two, a labourer, his cute cuticles caked with plaster, like clean white dirt, whom I met, the very day after my night with Gaetan, when we were both queueing to buy kebabs in the Latin Quarter. A nice, impressionable boy, no conversation, his head enhaloed by a frizz of blond pubic hair – the sex fairish, not truly memorable, except that I still find myself wondering what's become of him. There was Thadée, twenty-three, a masseur by profession but also an aspiring concert pianist, spotted reading an unusually little book at a lonely café table. Before we settled down to make very decent love, he played Debussy's *Clair de lune* on my naked shoulder-blades (*omoplates* – my favourite French word). And there was Jake, an American, twenty-five, whom I accosted at midnight just outside his hotel in the rue Bonaparte when I heard him drunkenly cursing his 'fucking so-called boyfriend'. He took me to his third-floor room up an ill-lit stairway as precarious as a rope ladder, switched on the light, turned round to look me properly up and down and, before I myself had time to follow him inside from the landing, said, 'Sorry. My mistake. No hard feelings?' – speak for yourself, buster! – and closed the door in my face.

There was naughty Enrique, Spanish, nineteen, as untiring as a pet pup with a slobbery tennis ball that, a session of throwing and fetching and throwing and fetching and throwing and fetching having finally come, from the human point of view, to its long overdue end, treats his exhausted master – in this instance, me – to a 'That's it?' moue of doggy ingratitude. There was Barrie, Schuyler's Barrie, whom I ran into by chance at a Francis Bacon exhibition at the Petit Palais and who, now in funds, stood me to a scrumptious dinner at the three-star Grand Véfour, a treat I felt obliged to reciprocate the only way I could afford. Sex dire – 'quipped' an apologetic if unembarrassed Barrie, God's little wiseacre, 'When I was your age, honey-chile, I'd wake up limp all over and stiff in one place. Now I wake up stiff all over and limp in one place.' (I did discover, however, that his advances to Schuyler, made two decades earlier, had all been rejected.) There was Italo, Italian, twenty-seven, melodramatically flaring nostrils, a coal-black kiss curl on either side of his brow, a raven's wing forelock that every five minutes would flop forward into his eyes, a clean-shaven pubic area that interested me strangely and a bottom-drawer collection of von Gloeden's photographs. There was Paul, just twenty, a fragile, tickly, nail-biting creature as confused about his sexuality as I'd been at sixteen. In the Voltaire, where I had him, I sucked his purplish penis as cautiously as a Murano glass-blower, desirous as I was to avoid spilling the tears that seemed about to lap over on to the lashes of his opalescent eyes. There was rich Sumner, forty-two, a Boston *rentier* with a champagne-coloured toy poodle that primly trotted ahead of us on points like a baby ballerina. Though he was the Paris-is-my-playground type of American I despise, he was not only staying at L'Hôtel, the hotel in which Wilde died, but also in Mistinguett's room with its glass Art Deco bed, a dual temptation I couldn't resist. As the sex was even direr than with Barrie, though, I'd have nodded off had not a multiplicity of glinting reflections of Lolita, the poodle, snoozing fitfully at the foot of the bed kept me awake long enough to see her master surreptitiously don a frilly black sleeping-mask and a hairnet. And there was Didier, finally a Didier to call my own, twenty-two and a tad too tattooed for my taste, but, oh my lord, what an athlete, what an acrobat! First, he would stand before me, starkers, cock and balls tucked out of sight behind his closed thighs, the bowdlerised edition of a boy. Then he'd stretch out on the

145

bed, double-jointedly drawing his now arched thighs back over his head and spreading his buttocks, with their high, Gene-Tierneyesque cheekbones, as far apart as they'd go. Then he'd knot his feet behind his neck and curl the palms of his hands round their soles, so that the tumerous mushroom of his balls sprouted from the crack in his backside like a single orb so neat and spherical and bursting with goodies you wanted to topknot the whole delicious doodad with a pretty pink velvet ribbon. And then, with an almost maternal gentleness and grace that was the very last thing I expected from him, he would ease us both into the *soixante-neuf* posture, my cock sliding like a thermometer into his mouth, his simultaneously into mine, as though our bodies were a pair of adjacent pieces of a jigsaw puzzle or a do-it-yourself kit to love.

During this busy period I was screwed on leaky, punctured, discoloured mattresses laid out any old how on uncarpeted floors (lots of these); in chintzy double beds whose Habitat bedspreads were topped off by the same three suede cushions in lozenge-patterned symmetry – grey, beige and buff-yellow; in tiny, cramped cots shoved into corner nooks of *chambres de bonne*; in bathtubs; on the carpet; in Mistinguett's bed, as I said; under a poster of a moody Jimmy Dean mooning along a rainswept New York street one blurry dawn a long, long time ago; on the lower berth of a multicoloured barge moored near the Seine's mini-Statue of Liberty; in a curvacious, queen-sized *lit-bateau* over whose polished cherry-wood head glowered a big black Soulages; once on a hammock; a half-dozen times atop that chafing San Andreas faultline that can never quite be smoothed over and forgotten about when hotel twin beds are pushed together to create what you hope will feel like a single one; on a sofa made from, of all things, Turkish saddle-bags (my dear, how too madly sweaty!); on many ordinary sofas; on the kind of outsize brass bed – my wrists and ankles roped tight to its four posts – against which, in satin scanties, Liz Taylor was once to be seen steamily draping herself on the poster of a Tennessee Williams movie; and, but always as a last resort, in my own snug little hotel-room bunk.

And there, reader, you have the end of my story, more or less. It's exactly fifty-six days since I started writing it – the first was the day after my night with Didier and today is the fifty-seventh. When I complete the few paragraphs I need to round it off, I shall send the manuscript to my cousin Dennis. I wouldn't entrust it to Mick, who, if I know him, would subject it first to a major 'creative' editing job, especially where his own portrait is concerned. Nor to my parents who, like most nice people, hold horrible views on the subject of homosexuality, regarding it as merely a less malignant variety of Aids. For them, as a gay man, something they must realise I am, I already *have* Aids. It just hasn't manifested itself yet. No, as I made clear in my very first paragraph, it will be up to Dennis to decide whether or not to try to get this memoir published. It won't be a quick or easy decision for him to arrive at. After all, he himself makes a brief cameo appearance in it under his own name – a cameo, Dennis, I'd rather you didn't censor – which means that, if it's to come out in book form, he too will be forced to 'come out' along with it. If, then, it happens at all, it may not happen for some time.

I still teach at the Berlitz but, except for the source material that it's provided me with for this memoir, it's ceased to offer me much more than paid employment. To be sure, there's still Schuyler, inescapable, irreplaceable Schuyler, now presiding over a common room of teachers fewer and fewer of whom he knows, and fewer and fewer of whom know either him or even what the noun 'doyen' means. Schuyler, I say to myself as I contemplate him, *you* at least never change. If only that constancy of yours, that presence and permanence, that physical and mental homogeneity, could rub off on the rest of us. Good health, unfortunately, is not contagious, which is perhaps the single thing most amiss with the world.

Ferey has gone for good. Is he still in France? Alive or dead? Nobody can tell me. Ralph Macavoy too. Just like that – one day there, the next not. (It shames me to admit it but, along with my genuine sorrow at his disappearance, as well as my sincere anxieties about the state of his health, I was chagrined to have to acknowledge to myself once and for all that I was never now going to know how well-hung he was.) And, or so Schuyler informed me, Peter, the garrulous, shaven-headed American whose good fortune it was forever to reside next door to the best *charcuterie* or *boulangerie* in Paris, has returned to the States to enter some sort of a Catholic retreat in New Hampshire. An ominous sign, I think.

Mick and I continue to see each other. Occasionally, when he's too exhausted to attend one of those ever more frequent meetings of his, usually held in a dilapidated church hall or youth club backroom out in some distant, dingy, double-digit arrondissement (every time I accompany him, it feels as though we have to travel farther and farther from the city centre), he'll invite me to spend an evening at home with him in his rue Daguerre apartment. We'll turn off all the lights, place a couple of candlesticks on the floor just out of elbow-shot, switch on TV (French television – putrid, but who cares), and, he stretching along the sofa on his tummy with his plate beneath him on the carpet, I resting my feet on the comfy and surprisingly sexy small of his back, we'll end up weeping into our linguine while watching, let's say, some whiskery old Gaby Morlay *mélo* or a dubbed BBC documentary about orphaned baby orangutans.

Though fading, Mick hasn't yet given up the ghost. He once quoted Madame du Barry to me. 'Just a few seconds more, executioner, please!' she was said to have pleaded on the scaffold. Even in the shadow of the guillotine life is better than death.

As for me, all I can do is await the inevitable. I can imagine what lies ahead for me, but I remain curiously unafraid and, when all is said and done, *I asked for it*. So much of my life heretofore has been a sham that I'd welcome even a fatal dose of reality.

If you find that hard to credit, you should know that it was actually at the very height of my sexual spree, my libidinal binge, that I first let my mind play over the implications of the risks I was quite consciously running. Such at any rate were those I'd already run by then, I could no longer doubt what their consequences would be. And there were nights when – after my current bedmate (whichever one he was) and I had slaked our thirst for one another's body and, incapable of sleep, I'd continue to feast on his slumbering, unsuspecting nakedness, sniffing his armpits, drawing a beguiled finger through the dank, shit-scented snarl of his ass-hair, stroking his shrivelled post-coital cock and feeling it wearily stiffen to my touch – there were nights, I say, when I'd catch myself rewinding in my head the chronology of all my fugitive encounters, straining to fashion a mental image of my partners' family tree, as it were, trying to figure out which one of those partners (and I had a few theories) was likeliest to have, like a card sharp, palmed the ace of spades, the ace of Aids, off on me.

The exercise, of course, was foredoomed to failure. And I was reminded of a tango I used to hear on the *Soledad*'s tinny hi-fi system (the *Soledad* was one of the discos I mentioned earlier, to which I was taken by Ferey). It was a derivative little melody, slower than most and of low priority in the pre-recorded medley of numbers whose unaltered sequence I grew as familiar with as the succession of tracks on some repeatedly listened-to LP. Its title was 'Buenas Noches Buenos Aires' and it told the tale of a lonely sailor reminiscing about the many women he'd bedded in the eponymous city and wondering which of them would bear him the son who would, in turn, bear his name when he died, as he was persuaded he one day would, at sea. I recall thinking how much I resembled that sailor, save that it's I who have been – as I'm certain I have been – impregnated (a word, I assure you, reader, that I weighed long before using). I resemble him, too, in having absolutely no regrets.

So – Kim, Edouard, Didier, Enrique, Gaetan, Barbet, *mes semblables, mes frères*, all those members of the only set, the only family, the only brotherhood, to which I've ever felt I truly belonged or wished to belong, all those of you with whom I've been privileged to share the splendours and miseries, grandeur and servitude, of the homosexual condition, let me salute you fraternally, wherever you are.

I don't want to die – naturally, I don't – but, if I must, then I've now come to realise how proud I'd be, how utterly unashamed, to die of Aids.

No, I take that back. To die of AIDS.